NORSE MYTHOLOGY FOR BOSTONIANS

ROWDY GEIRSSON is the author of *The Scandinavian Aggressors*, an offbeat odyssey that explores the freezing heart of the modern Northlands. His writing on the Northlands has additionally appeared in *Medieval World: Culture and Conflict*, the American-Scandinavian Foundation's *Scandinavian Review*, and the Sons of Norway's *Viking Magazine*. He writes *McSweeney's* longest-running humor column, was the first American to appear opposite Amon Amarth's frontman on the *Grimfrost* podcast, and is the sole proprietor of *www.scandinavianaggression.com*, a mediocre blog about vikings past and present. Follow him on Xitter @RGeirsson, BS @rgeirsson.bsky.social and/or on Instadamn @rowdygeirsson, or don't.

Norse Mythology
for Bostonians

A Transcription of the Impudent Edda

Transcribed with an Introduction and Notes by
ROWDY GEIRSSON

PUFFIN CARCASS

PUFFIN CARCASS

An Imprint of Scandinavian Aggression
www.scandinavianaggression.com

Portions of this book first appeared online at
McSweeney's Internet Tendency in a slightly different form.

Lyrics from *Song to Hall Up High*, words and music by Thomas Börje Forsberg,
copyright © 1990. All rights reserved.

Lyrics from *Dirty Water*, words and music by Edward C. Cobb,
copyright © 1965. All rights reserved.

The Dvergatal is reprinted from *The Poetic Edda* translated by Lee M. Hollander,
2nd edition, revised, copyright © 1962, renewed 1990. Courtesy of the University of Texas Press.

Manufacturing via IngramSpark
Book design by Rowdy Geirsson
Third Edition 2025

Library of Congress Cataloging-in-Publication Data

Names: Geirsson, Rowdy
Title: Norse Mythology for Bostonians:
A Transcription of the Impudent Edda
Description: First Edition | Norumbega: Scandinavian Aggression
Subjects: Mythology, Norse, Edda, Scandinavia, Vikings,
Boston, Massachusetts, New England, Impudence.

ISBN: 978-0-578-58652-6

Puffin Carcass
An imprint of
Scandinavian Aggression
Norumbega, Vinland
www.scandinavianaggression.com

"I know you watch over me
Father of all the past
And all that will ever be
You are the first and the last

The watcher of all that lives
The guardian of all that died

The one-eyed god way up high
Who rules my world and the sky

Northern wind take my song up high
To the hall of glory in the sky
So its gates shall greet me open wide
When my time has come to die"

   —Quorthon / Bathory,
   Song to Hall Up High

"I'm gonna tell you a story
I'm gonna tell you about my town
I'm gonna tell you a big fat story, baby
It's all about my town

Yeah, down by the river
Down by the banks of the river the Charles
That's where you'll find me
Along with the lovers, muggers, and thieves

Well, I love that dirty water
Oh, Boston you're my home"

   —Larry Tamblyn / The Standells,
   Dirty Water

Contents

Contents

*Asterisks indicate myths that are wholly unique to
The Impudent Edda and not corroborated by earlier sources

For Leifr Eiríksson
Discoverer of Vinland
Colonizer of Norumbega

In loving memory
~970 – ~1020

Introduction

The classic tales of Norse mythology have entertained men, women, and children for centuries, albeit in very different capacities and formats as time has passed and society has evolved. While stories such as Odin's belligerent murder of a greedy witch or Thor's cross-dressing misadventure with evil frost giants may have always provided a certain degree of entertainment value through the ages regardless of time period or culture, they also significantly shaped and guided the daily lives of the pre-Christian Scandinavians who originated them. These stories occupied a central role in the spiritual beliefs of the Vikings, and the Norsemen and women who stayed behind at home while their brethren went off plundering and colonizing overseas.[1] It was only with the gradual Christianization of Scandinavia during the four centuries that straddled the year 1000 that the importance of the Norse gods among the Scandinavians faded, though the stories of their lewd, immature, and occasionally heroic exploits lived on and were eventually preserved in the written word.

"Edda" is the term that has come to be given to each of the three primary sources containing the original stories of Norse mythology. The fantastical stories preserved in the Eddas have become increasingly popular in recent decades, especially as mod-

---

1   It is a common present-day misunderstanding that all Norsemen and women were Vikings. This is incorrect, as only the medieval Scandinavians who sailed away from home to attack far-away cities or colonize distant lands were considered Vikings in their day. All Vikings were Norse (or assimilated into the Norse culture, if not originally Norse), but not all Norse were Vikings.

ern translations and technological advances have enabled them to reach larger and larger audiences. They have served as substantial sources of inspiration for many great writers, artists, and composers. Prominent figures such as Richard Wagner, Henry Wadsworth Longfellow, JRR Tolkien (and consequently most other contemporary fantasy novelists and game developers), and Quorthon (of Swedish death metal fame) all borrowed and embellished on the original Eddic material to bring their own creative visions to life. As a result, and thanks in particular to the global audience reached by *The Lord of the Rings* and *The Hobbit* film franchises in the 21st century, the average non-Norse person is now more familiar than ever with the iconography of Norse mythology, even if he or she is not fully aware of it.[2]

It is also important, if somewhat ironic, to note that each of the Eddas themselves were simply the culmination of a grand, oral—not written—tradition in which the stories of Odin, Thor, and all the others were passed down from generation to generation for centuries. As such, these stories certainly varied over distance as well as over time throughout the Nordic region. Thus, it is highly unlikely, for example, that the version of the story about the trickster god, Loki, tying his own hairy scrotum to a goat's beard and then playing tug of war with it was the same in Sweden around the year 900 as it was in Greenland two centuries later, if the story even existed in both places/time periods at all. As the collective repository of most Norse mythology, the Eddas provide only a very limited window into what must have once been a much more robust and nuanced mythology than that to which we are presently afforded insight today.

In addition to the Eddas themselves, short mythological tales and references also exist in the worn pages of other medieval

---

2   One familiar example for the average movie-goer is that of
     Smaug, the cruel and lazy dragon from *The Hobbit*, who was
     blatantly modeled after the dragons that appear in ancient
     Norse literature—right down to the hoard of gold and
     demonic-speaking abilities. Tolkien very deliberately based
     many aspects of his writings on the characters, themes, and
     environments found in the myths and sagas of the Norse-
     men.

manuscripts. *Flateyjarbók*, the heftiest of ancient Icelandic man-uscripts, contains a wealth of saga material and some mytho-logical material, as does the *Gesto Danorum*, the ancient histo-ry of the Danes, written by Saxo Grammaticus, although in his work the gods are presented as evil-doing mortals rather than immature but divine beings. Many other manuscripts have also preserved stories that shed light on ancient Norse thought and beliefs such as the *Völsunga Saga* and *Hrólfs Saga Kraka*, and while these certainly help to paint a fuller picture of the known aspects of Norse mythology, they nonetheless typically focus on the earthly exploits of mortal men and women rather than those of the gods. The Eddas thus remain the main primary sources devoted specifically to the deeds of the gods and in that sense they are invaluable.

The two earliest Eddas were recorded in Iceland in the thir-teenth century and were the culmination of that country's long tradition of oral story-telling. The first of these Eddas was long thought to have been transcribed by a monk known as Saemun-dr Sigfusson the Wise (though now there is some contention about the authorship) and is known by many names: *The Codex Regius*, *The Saemundr Edda*, *The Eldest Edda* (formerly *The Elder Edda*), and most commonly, *The Poetic Edda*, because the bulk of its contents are written in poetic verse. The Norse people, as with most other ancient and medieval peoples, loved poetry and generally chose to relate their stories in long, complicated poetic verses for eager audiences. The more complicated and ornate the poem, the more respected the story-teller, or "skald" as Norse poets were called in their day.

The second Edda was written by Snorri Sturluson, a conniv-ing and devious scoundrel who enjoyed a great degree of power and prosperity during his lifetime. As the most prominent land-holder and politician in Iceland during the late twelfth and ear-ly thirteenth centuries, he was prone to dreaming up traitorous schemes from the comfort of his own private hot-spring hot tub until one day his enemies gathered at his house, broke in, and murdered him while he grovelled in the basement. In addition to instigating blood feuds and pronouncing the laws of the land,[3]

---

3   During his lifetime, Snorri was elected to serve as the Ice-

Snorri also collected manuscripts and wrote many of his own, including the original history of Norway.[4] However, he is best known for his Edda, appropriately enough called *Snorri's Edda*, *The Middle-Child Edda* (formerly *The Younger Edda*), and *The Prose Edda*.[5] While Snorri wrote this Edda in prose, rather than poetic format, he nonetheless referenced and borrowed many of the same verses that appear in *The Poetic Edda*. Both Eddas are preserved and on exhibit at the Árni Magnússon Institute for Icelandic Studies in Reykjavik.[6]

The third Edda was recorded somewhat more recently during the early twenty-first century, specifically on June 12, 2019, in Boston, Massachusetts. In a drastic departure in terms of recording method in comparison to the two earlier Icelandic Eddas, this Edda was not hand-written in a fine, graceful script on parchment or vellum, but rather was audibly recorded on a mobile telephone device and found abandoned in an alleyway behind a local bar next to a puddle of piss in the city's famously angry, Celtic neighborhood colloquially known as "Southie." The author remains

---

landic Lawspeaker twice. The role of the Lawspeaker was to officiate the proceedings of the Icelandic Althing, the oldest parliament in the world. Primary duties consisted of reciting the laws of the land and serving as an arbitrator of disputes, which frequently involved the irresponsible and reckless grazing of sheep, and ruthless murders.

4   In addition to his Edda, Snorri was also the author of *Heimskringla*, known in English as *The History of the Kings of Norway*.

5   To add to the confusion, *The Prose Edda* has survived in a total of four different manuscripts, the most substantial of which is referred to as the *Codex Regius*, which is also one of the names for *The Poetic Edda*. The more common titles of *The Prose Edda* and *The Poetic Edda* (or Elder Eddas when referred to collectively), however, will be used exclusively and consistently throughout this edition of *The Impudent Edda*.

6   Other copies of *The Prose Edda* exist in Denmark, Sweden, and the Netherlands, but the copy in Iceland is the oldest, most complete, and most famous.

The dank alley in South Boston where archaeologists discovered the only extant copy of The Impudent Edda.

unknown to this day, but thanks to the remarkable preservative properties of non-biodegradable digital technology, this Edda survived the damaging passage of time and weather and has since come to be regarded—though not without some dispute as will be discussed further below—as the most important find relating to Norse mythology and pagan spiritual beliefs since the exhumation of the Oseberg Ship in 1904-1905.[7] As with the other two Elder Eddas before it, it has taken on many names, including: *The Youngest Edda*, *The Infant(ile) Edda*, *The Wicked Retarded Edda*, *Some Dumb Masshole's Edda*, and most commonly, *The Impudent*

---

7   The Oseberg ship was exhumed in 1904-1905 in Vestfold, Norway. It was a remarkable find, containing numerous grave goods in excellent condition. The ship itself has become the basis for the world's collective imagination regarding the ideal appearance of a standard Viking sea-going vessel, replete with dragon-headed prow.

Edda. As with the Icelandic Eddas, this Edda is also on exhibit and may be viewed in all of its cracked-touch-screen splendor at the Museum of Bad Art, which is housed in the drab basement of a small, independent movie theater in Somerville, Massachusetts. Aside from some unabridged yet incomplete snippets archived online,[8] the volume that you now hold in your hands is the very first transcription of *The Impudent Edda* to be released for the general public.

As with the elder *Poetic* and *Prose Eddas*, *The Impudent Edda* was composed in the vernacular of its time and place. It does not feature the complex arrangements of wordplay and meter as found in *The Poetic Edda*, nor does it feature the tense, often direct and to-the-point styling of *The Prose Edda*. Rather, *The Impudent Edda* meanders its way through a series of loosely connected events in the days of the lives of the Norse gods in a sort of stream of consciousness that would make Massachusetts native Jack Kerouac proud. *The Impudent Edda* is contemporary to its time and place, just as the *Poetic* and *Prose Eddas* were to theirs.

The transcription presented here is just that—a transcription. This is not a translation into standard modern English. The original language of *The Impudent Edda* is similar enough to both the contemporary American and British dialects that a translation was not deemed necessary for readers fluent in English, just as the same is true of the language found in the original Elder Edda manuscripts for present-day Icelandic readers.[9] And just as the Elder Eddas feature notes and commentaries written by Saemundr (or the unknown scribe, if not him) and Snorri respectively in the margins of the original tomes, so too is the original copy of *The Impudent Edda* laden with frequent asides and outbursts, which have not been included here. The decision to eliminate the side commentary from this edition of *The Impudent Edda* is addressed in more detail in the section of introductory material entitled, *A Note on the Linguistics and Method of Transcription*.

---

8   These snippets may be accessed by visiting
    https://www.mcsweeneys.net/columns/norse-history-for-bostonians.

9   Unlike English, the Icelandic language has not changed
    much in the past one thousand years.

The tales of the Norse myths have been preserved, illustrated, and re-written down for centuries. While such manuscripts have not typically contributed new mythological knowledge beyond that found in the Elder Eddas, the arrival of The Impudent Edda *has invited scholars the rare opportunity for new interpretations of some of this older content, such as this image of Odin from an 18th century Icelandic manuscript. Is Odin simply wearing ornate, old-timey garb as has long been assumed to be the case? Or did an unknown Icelandic scribe from 300 years ago accurately foretell his future sports team allegiances? These questions, and others, remain open for future study.*

In terms of content, *The Impudent Edda* follows the two Elder Eddas closely in the overall mythic story arc—the creation of the world, the adolescent behavior featuring the sex-crazed and temper-tantrum-fueled trials and tribulations of the gods, and the complete and utter destruction of the world and almost everything in it by a relentless fire at the end of time. There are, however, a number of substantial deviations that occur in the actual transpiring of certain events, as well as the inclusion of a handful of episodes that occur neither in *The Poetic Edda* nor *The Prose Edda*. Similarly, those two Eddas contain certain episodes that are missing from *The Impudent Edda*. The same may be said of the other primary sources containing mythological material, such as the aforementioned *Flateyjarbók* or *Völsunga Saga*. All of this is to be expected given that each source is nothing more than a very narrow snapshot of the specific version of Norse mythology that existed in the specific era and place in which it was recorded, with each authors' own biases and prejudices present in the recording. The most substantial of these discrepancies have been addressed in the footnotes of the text of this transcription.

As mentioned above, the legitimacy of *The Impudent Edda* has been disputed, most frequently by members of the academic establishment. Many scholars of mythology and medieval or comparative literature have questioned the authenticity of the Edda, citing the inability to verify its origin, the lack of supporting contextual archeological material, and its inconsistencies with the two Elder Eddas. Proponents of *The Impudent Edda*, which include many armchair folklorists and online lifestyle gurus, conversely argue that while its legitimacy cannot be proven, neither can it be disproven. The proponents are usually quick to point out that this is not a repeat of the Kensington Runestone incident[10] and that no one is postulating that *The Impudent Edda* is

---

10 The Kensington Runestone incident was initiated in 1898
     when farmer Olof Ohman discovered what he claimed to be
     an original Norse runestone in Douglas County, Minnesota
     dating to the 14th century. The stone has been studied and its
     authenticity debated ever since. The majority of the scholarly community generally considers it to be a hoax because
     linguistic analysis has revealed that the language carved into

The Kensington Runestone. Early evidence of Scandinavian involvement in Minnesota, or hoax?

an authentic medieval document that has survived the same passage of time as the Elder Eddas. Experts all agree that *The Impudent Edda* is multiple centuries younger and that it was recorded in a time and place quite different from those of the Elder Eddas.

Additionally, and as was mentioned at the beginning of this introduction, Norse pagan beliefs certainly dwindled drastically with the conversion to Christianity in Scandinavia, but there is reason to believe that they may have never been stamped out completely. Small numbers of Scandinavians continued to worship Thor, Odin, and Frey's enormous penis in secret long after the coming of Christianity to the Nordic region. This is particularly

----

the surface of the stone is not identical to the familiar Old Swedish as is found in other, contemporaneous artefacts from the old country, but the verdict remains inconclusive.

well-documented in the case of Iceland,[11] but it is also believed to be true of the other Scandinavian countries as well. The extent to which these pagan customs continued to be practiced is unknown, but it remains entirely plausible that the stories and beliefs of the old gods may have evolved over that course of time and eventually made their way to Boston via Worcester, Massachusetts, which was a major destination for Swedish immigrants in the 19th century.

Furthermore, much like wicca, Ásatrú[12] has been on the rise now for decades, with believers of the old ways coming out of the dark in increasing numbers. Ásatrú's presence in New England is not documented in the historical record prior to the loosening of social norms that occurred during the latter half of the 20th century and the question remains as to whether the beliefs and customs associated with the pagan religion were ever present in the Commonwealth prior to the cultural revolution or not. Is *The Impudent Edda* the first instance of Ásatrú beliefs found in Massachusetts, long kept secret, to have emerged from the prevailing Anglo-Saxon Protestant and Irish/Italian Catholic shadows into the light of day? Do the stories that it contains provide genuine evidence of a more evolved, heretofore unknown version of Norse mythology than was previously preserved in medieval Iceland? Or is it all just complete bullshit?

The debate continues, unresolved. The purpose of this transcription is not to argue the case one way or the other, but rather to provide the general public with access to material that has never before been available. The Elder Eddas have been available to the general English-speaking public in various translations for decades, and now for the first time ever *The Impudent Edda* joins their ranks. The reader is invited to come to his or her own conclusion.

---

11 In the year 1000, Iceland voted to become a Christian nation, but continued to allow the worship of the pagan gods among its populace, provided that such practice only occurred in the privacy of the home.

12 Also known as Odinism or Heathenry, Ásatrú is a present-day pagan religion that revolves around the Norse gods, including customs reminiscent of ancient Norse pagan rituals, minus the human and animal sacrificial slaughter.

A Note on the Linguistics and Method of Transcription

As mentioned in the *Introduction*, *The Impudent Edda* was originally preserved as an oral recording on a lost and forgotten cell phone. Because the Edda was recorded in this manner rather than the more commonly employed written word, it becomes an impossible task for the listener to overlook the distinct vernacular inherent to its locality: the Boston dialect of contemporary American English. This particularity has lent *The Impudent Edda* its own unique flavor and imbued it with a richness of wordplay that would surely dissipate if an effort to translate it into standard American English had been undertaken. Partly for this reason and partly because Bostonian is comprehensible to the vast majority of the English-speaking public, the transcription provided here has been faithfully executed in the vernacular dialect of the original recording.

To assist in the readability of the transcription, spelling and grammatical rules have been adapted from proper American English, standardized, and applied methodically throughout the text. The reader will quickly notice the non-rhoticity of the Bostonian letter "r" in the text, as well as other particularities related to the Bostonian dialect. Certain rare exceptions, however, have been made in the adaptation of American English to Bostonian. These pertain to a small handful of proper nouns, which have maintained their standard American spelling. This was done to avoid confusion for the reader in those instances where the improper Bostonian spelling may have lacked clarity, or the standard American spelling is so commonplace that it did not make sense to adjust it. One prominent example is the spelling of Thor's name, which has been maintained as "Thor" rather than the more properly Bostonian alternative of "Tho-wah."

Also as previously mentioned in the *Introduction*, *The Impudent Edda* contains many asides and outbursts throughout the entirety of its recording that deviate from the telling of the actual myths themselves, such as that which occurs mid-way through the story about Odin excreting mead while flying through the sky after having shape-shifted into the form of an eagle:

> "Come on, Tuuka!
> This is fuckin' bullshit fahr fuck's sake!"

This sort of extraneous material has been edited out of this edition because it was deemed irrelevant, as well as to improve the flow of the narrative.

Old Norse Astrophysics

The Norse gods inhabited a universe held together by a very different set of astrophysical properties than those that inform our collective understanding of the cosmos today. The gap[1] between these two schools of thought is so incredibly vast that they are essentially irreconcilable, and while one need not possess full comprehension of each and every astrophysical property that courses through the Norse myths, a fundamental grasp of the conceptual framework is useful to properly appreciate them. A brief overview is therefore provided here in modern scientific parlance for the casual contemporary reader.

Rather than an expanding and accelerating universe that consists of all space, time, matter, and energy and that was itself formed in the wake of a particularly forceful singularity at the beginning of all time, the Old Norse concept of the universe consists of a constant single, high-energy interstellar structure that has always been and always will be.[2] Known as Yggdra-

---

1   A rhetorical gap, not to be confused with the Ginnungagap, which is addressed on page 3 in the first chapter of the main text, *Cosmological Frost Giant Genocide*.

2   There is some debate and ambiguity surrounding the eternal nature of Yggdrasil as asserted by the Eddas. In the *Völuspá*, the opening poem of *The Poetic Edda*, an unsubstantiated claim is made that Yggdrasil, in the earliest era of the universe's existence, was in fact formed from a forceful gravitational singularity, much like the Big Bang, resulting in an ash seedling bursting forth into mature, wooden splendor from the ripened black hole in which it was planted. The *Prose* and *Impudent Eddas* do not verify this, and the notes

sil, this interstellar structure exhibits a visible electromagnetic spectrum that resembles the form of an enormous ash tree with three asymptotic giant branches forming its roots while numerous high-luminosity evolutionary model protoplanetary nebulae constitute the likeness of its leafy limbs. Instances of large-scale gamma radiation have been observed at Yggdrasil's extremities, particularly at one of its asymptotic giant branches where a single long-duration gamma-ray burst known as Níðhöggr the Dragon augments the cosmic radioactive decay rate by nibbling upon it at the molecular level.

Yggdrasil's branch-like protoplanetary nebulae are afflicted by high-order magnitude sub-pockets of interstellar dust and gas within four distinct high-latitude diffuse molecular clouds, creating dense clump formations on its non-ionized plasmic leaves and negatively impacting Yggdrasil's coefficient of photosynthesis. Within the Old Norse school of thought, these molecular clouds are known as Dáinn, Dvalinn, Duneyrr, and Duraþrór and are often depicted as four aggressive male deers ravenously chomping away at the extraterrestrial leaf-flesh of the known universe.

Also detected among Yggdrasil's protoplanetary nebulae is an unnamed binary neutron star system, the hostile pulsar of which emits highly magnetized electromagnetic radiation which is transmitted as a series of avian insults via a squirrel-like forbidden mechanism known as Ratatosk that undergoes a spontaneous spin-flip transition, freefalling at the speed of light and restabilizing among Yggdrasil's asymptotic giant branches where the radioactive avian insults are absorbed by Níðhöggr the Dragon, resulting in a sharp upward spike of the Dragon's already highly excited state. Níðhöggr reacts to this increase of energy through a series of rapid-inimical non-thermal ophidian invectives that are redshifted towards Ratatosk and re-transmitted through the spectral line to the unnamed hostile pulsar. This antagonistic interstellar exchange of energy continues for all eternity, even after the rest of the universe is destroyed in the catastrophic cosmic fire of one final, massive supernova explosion known as Ragnarök.

---

throughout the text of this transcription take the stance that Yggdrasil was considered truly eternal in Old Norse thought.

A Brief Overview of the 9 Worlds

Within the Old Norse school of astrophysical thought, nine primary life-supporting atmospheric systems were believed to exist within the interstellar structure of Yggdrasil's ash tree-like framework. Each system possessed its own unique characteristics and served as host to its own uniquely evolved, native species of lifeforms. The 9 Worlds as they were known among the Norse are as follows:

Asgard: Home to the primary tribe of gods known as the Aesir, Asgard is located on the luminous spectrum of the uppermost of Yggdrasil's three asymptotic giant branches. Essentially a fortress, Asgard is surrounded by massive, stone walls to keep its enemies out. Within the protection of these walls may be found the individual halls and hang-out places of the gods, such as Valhalla (Odin's hall of the slain), Fensalir (Frigg's salon in the Back Bay), and Sökkvabekkr (where Sága seduces married gods into having extramarital affairs). Asgard is connected to Middle-Earth by Bifrost, the magnificent rainbow bridge.

Elf World: Known as Alfheim in earlier sources, Elf World is located among a different magnitude of the luminous spectrum of the same asymptotic giant branch as Asgard. As its name suggests, Elf World is home to the elves.

Dwarf World: Known as Svartelfheim in earlier sources, Dwarf World is a damp and dark place located beneath the ground of Middle-Earth.

Giant Land: Known as Jotunheim in earlier sources, Giant Land is located among the mid-level asymptotic branch of Yggdrasil, due east of Middle-Earth on the luminous scale. Giant Land is a cold and forbidding place, full of mountains. As its name suggests, it is the home to frost giants and mountain giants, but not fire giants.

Hel: The grim, gray land of the dead that awaits those who do not die in battle and is presided over by the demoness with the same name, Hel. Located near, or within, Niflheim along the third and lowest asymptotic branch of Yggdrasil.

Middle-Earth: Also known as Midgard, Middle-Earth is located among the mid-level giant asymptotic branch of Yggdrasil and is the home of humans. Encircled by a vast ocean, Middle-Earth is nonetheless connected to Asgard by Bifrost, the rainbow bridge.

Muspellsheim: The land of fire and home of fire giants, it is unclear exactly where Muspellsheim is located within Yggdrasil's interstellar structure, but it is a hot and evil place. The heat from Muspellsheim melted the ice of Niflheim from which all life in the universe subsequently arose.

Niflheim: A dark, misty world of ice and cold, Niflheim is located along the luminous spectrum of Yggdrasil's lowest asymptotic branch. Once devoid of life, it is now populated by Hel and her army of undead zombies. Niflheim is located in dangerously close proximity to the radioactive decay emanating from the long-duration gamma-ray burst known as Níðhöggr the Dragon.

Vanaheim: Home to the secondary tribe of gods known as the Vanir, Vanaheim, like Asgard, is located along the luminous spectrum of Yggdrasil's uppermost asymptotic branch.

OTHER PLACES OF INTEREST

Folkvangr: Freyja's flowery meadow located in Asgard, where she receives her share of fallen warriors as delivered by the valkyries.

Ginnungagap: The primordial abyss that was located somewhere along the luminous spectrum of Yggdrasil's mid-level asymptotic giant branch at a magnitude between those of Niflheim and Muspellsheim.

Hvergelmir: Located beneath Niflheim, Hvergelmir is the spring source of all water throughout the cosmos and home to numerous, nasty snakes.

Iron Wood: Also known as Járnviðr, Iron Wood lies somewhere east of Middle-Earth and is presided over by Angrboda, mother of the notorious monsters Fenrir, Jörmundgandr, and Hel, as well as many wolves. The forest is also populated by many evil troll women.

Valhalla: Odin's hall of the slain, Valhalla is located within the protected fortress walls of Asgard. It is a magnificent hall with 540 doors and a roof constructed of shields. At Valhalla, the Einherjar, Odin's fallen warriors, battle all day and feast all night, being served roast pork and fresh mead that flows freely from the udders of Heidrun, the magical mead-bearing goat. The Einherjar are waited upon by the very same valkyries who plucked them up off the battlefield.

Well of Mimir: Beneath Giant Land is the Well of Mimir, where Odin sometimes consults Mimir's decapitated head for advice.

Well of Urd: Located in the same luminous spectrum as Asgard is the Well of Urd, where the norns live, weaving the fate of all men and women.

Old Norse Racial Diversity

Having been populated almost entirely (if not fully) with nothing but pale, white people, medieval Scandinavia was not a very racially diverse place. However, the Scandinavians have always displayed a heightened degree of social awareness and thus they attempted to amend this deficiency in heterogeneity by populating their mythology with a whole array of unique races. An overview of those races is presented here, complete with all the enduring generalizations, insensitivities, and basic prejudices that one would fully expect to course through any such present-day discussion about a topic so timeless that it continues to incite and divide *Homo sapiens* even in the 21st century.

Dwarves: The dwarves are small, near-sighted creatures who live below ground in Dwarf World where they hoard gold and make magnificent jewelry. Sometimes referred to as dark-elves or black-elves, the dwarves are human-like in appearance, but much shorter, stockier, hairier, and uglier. Originally existing as maggots who burrowed under the skin of the primordial giant Ymir's cold, lifeless body, the dwarves were given human intelligence and their present physical form by Odin in one of his rare acts of sympathy and kindness.

Elves: The elves, sometimes called light-elves, are mystical, godlike beings, fair, tall, and pleasant in all ways. They possess magical abilities and live in Elf World but do not play a prominent role in *The Impudent Edda* or either of the Elder Eddas.

Giants: The antagonists of the gods. The giants existed before the gods, and are generally a hostile race, although some giants go renegade and become friendly allies of the gods. Massively large in size, the frost giants and mountain giants live in Giant Land while their even more evil brethren, the fire giants, live in Muspellsheim.

Gods and **Goddesses**: The protagonists of Norse mythology. The gods and goddesses are grim, fatalistic, sex-crazed, manipulative, and immature. Most of them are classified into one of two tribes:

> **Aesir**: The Aesir comprise the primary tribe of gods and goddesses, with a broad fixation on war, death, battle, poetry, and heavy drinking. Odin and Thor belong to this tribe of gods. The Aesir live in Asgard.

> **Vanir**: The Vanir are the secondary tribe of gods and goddesses, with a fixation on sex and physical attractiveness. Frey and Freyja belong to this tribe of gods. The Vanir live in Vanaheim.

In addition to the Aesir and Vanir, a handful of ambiguously divine beings also exist; their affiliations, as well as their genetics, are unknown. These figures skim a fine line between the gods and giants, frequently with mixed parentage from both races.

Norns: The norns are the weavers of fate who live beside the Well of Urd. There are three norns who have achieved superstar celebrity status: Urd (who shares the same name as the well that she lives beside), Verdandi, and Skuld, though there are many other norns, some of which are sweet and some of which are just downright nasty.

Ogres: See trolls.

Trolls: A generic, catch-all term for ambiguous, off-putting, and hostile beings that do not at first glance obviously belong to the race of giants. Trolls have a tendency to live far away from all forms of civilization, usually in forests or caves. Ogres may be seen as a species subset within the genus of troll.

Valkyries: Choosers of the slain, the valkyries ride through the sky plucking up fallen warriors on the battlefield to be taken either to Odin's hall of battle and glory, Valhalla, or to Freyja's flowery meadow, Folkvangr.

Prominent Figures of the Old Norse Pantheon

GODS AND GODDESSES: AESIR

Belichick: Known as Hermod in earlier sources, little is known of Belichick's personality other than that he is very bold and a great strategical thinker. A bastard son of Odin, his mother is unknown but is presumed to not be Frigg, Odin's wife.

Balder: See Brady.

Brady: Known as Balder and nicknamed the White or the Beautiful in earlier sources, Brady is the most attractive of the gods, as well as the most popular ever since he started playing quarterback for the New England Patriots. Brady is the one legitimate son of Odin and Frigg and is married to Gisele, known as Nanna in earlier sources, with whom he fathered, Forseti, a minor god who is reputed to be good at resolving legal disputes. Forseti receives passing mention in earlier sources but does not figure into *The Impudent Edda*.

Frigg: Considered to be particularly splendid in numerous ways that go unspecified, Frigg is foremost among the goddesses. Wife to Odin and mother to Brady/Balder, Frigg nonetheless lives apart in her own home in the fens, Fensalir, because no one can tolerate living with Odin 24/7, not even an all-powerful goddess.

Gisele: Known as Nanna in earlier sources, little is known about Gisele other than that she stems from German Brazilian heritage and that she previously made a living stunning onlookers with her amazing physique as she walked up and down the runway. She is also married to all-star quarterback/golden god Brady/Balder and she mothered Forseti, their otherwise non-descript lawyer son.

Hermod: See Belichick.

Hod: The blind god, a son of Odin and brother of Brady/Balder. It is uncertain who his mother is.

Hoenir: A lesser god in the Norse pantheon, Hoenir is known for being thick-skulled and none too bright. Sometimes he hangs out with Odin.

Idunn: Goddess and keeper of the magical apples of youth, which the gods and goddesses must all feed upon from time to time in order to stave off old age and thereby cheat death by natural causes. Idunn is married to Bragi, the most poetic of the gods with the possible exception of Odin. Bragi is a great story-teller but goes unmentioned in *The Impudent Edda*.

Mimir: A very wise god with a traumatically short life span.

Nanna: See Gisele.

Odin: The top dog of all the gods, also known as the All-Father for his fathering of all the world. Odin's wife is Frigg, with whom he fathered Brady/Balder. As a manipulative and un-faithful husband, Odin has also fathered many other bastard sons. One-eyed, wise, war-mongering, and grim, Odin has a penchant for poetry and enjoys instigating conflicts and wandering Middle-Earth disguised as a hobo. A pair of gos-siping ravens keep him company upon his throne, Hlidskjalf, from whence he watches over all the world with his all-seeing eye. In the evenings he entertains his army of undead Viking warriors in Valhalla with eternal battle, roast pork, and mead that flows freely from the magical udders of the divine goat, Heidrun.

Sága: The goddess who lives at Sökkvabekkr. She enjoys drinking and flirting with Odin and/or Thor (depending on the source).

Sigyn: The wife of Loki who presumably fell in love with him when she was very young and extremely foolish. Not much is known about Sigyn other than the role that she plays in the final days of the gods leading up to Ragnarök.

Sif: A goddess with lovely, flowing, golden hair. Sif is married to Thor, and together they begat Thrud, their daughter. From an earlier relationship during her reckless youth, Sif also became mother to Ull, a highly skilled skier and archer, but who does not figure into *The Impudent Edda*.

Thor: Son of Odin and Mother Earth, Thor is the strongest of all the gods. Boisterous and red-headed with a bushy beard, Thor can outdrink any other god and is proud of it. He routinely defends Asgard, the home of the gods, from the hostilities of evil giants with his mighty hammer, Mjölnir. Thor also enjoys journeying among the 9 Worlds, particularly with Loki for no apparent reason, and his hot temper often lands him in embarrassing situations. Thor is husband to golden-haired Sif, with whom he fathered their daughter Thrud. Through various extra-marital affairs, he has also fathered Magni and Modi, two strapping young lads born with the strength of Thor himself. None of Thor's children play a role in *The Impudent Edda*.

Tyr: The bravest and most fearless of the gods, Tyr is a one-handed bachelor who prefers battle to diplomacy. The son of the hostile giant, Hymir and his wife Hrod, it remains unclear how Tyr became an ally and well-respected member of the gods with such disastrous lineage.

GODS AND GODDESSES: VANIR

Frey: The chief god of the weather and fertility, which is somewhat ironic since he has no children of his own. Frey is the son of Njord and the twin brother of Freyja and is married to the giantess Gerd. His most distinct feature is his enormous penis, which is almost always erect.

Freyja: Probably the sluttiest of the goddesses, Freyja suffers a bad habit of selling her body for jewelry. As with her twin brother Frey, she is also associated with fertility and is generally considered to be the hottest and most sexually desirable of all the goddesses. She also has a dark side and is somewhat death-obsessed. Like Odin, she rules over a portion of the fallen warriors who die on the battlefield from her home beside the meadow known as Folkvangr, though her role in the afterlife is much less prominent. She is the daughter of Njord and the wife of Odr, who left her to go on travels while she stayed behind and cried tears of red gold. Prior to his departure, Odr and Freyja had a beautiful daughter, Hnoss, but neither Hnoss nor Odr receive mention in *The Impudent Edda*.

Kvasir: A divine being created from the spittle of the other gods, Kvasir is also, confusingly, regarded as the wisest of the Vanir.

Njord: God of the sea and wind, Njord is married to the mountain giant Skadi, though they live apart. Through a previous incestuous relationship with his unnamed sister, Njord is father to the sex-object god and goddess twins, Frey and Freyja.

AMBIGUOUSLY DIVINE BEINGS OF
UNKNOWN HERITAGE

Aegir: An ambiguously divine being, Aegir has been named as a giant but is often regarded as a god. He is the ruler of the seas, a magnificent host of wild underwater parties, and a mighty brewer of excellent craft beer. He is married to Ran, who enjoys drowning human seafarers but goes unmentioned in *The Impudent Edda*. Together, Aegir and Ran are parents to the waves.

Charlie: Another ambiguously divine being of unknown heritage, Charlie's lot is to ride forever on the T beneath the streets of Boston. His existence and role in the Norse myths is attested to only in *The Impudent Edda*.

Heimdall: The watchman of the gods, Heimdall lives near Bifrost, the rainbow bridge where he remains on constant vigilance against any enemies that might approach the homeland of the gods. He was given birth by nine mothers and is occasionally considered to be a member of the Vanir, though his genuine affiliation remains unclear. 20th century Norse religion expert, H.R. Ellis Davidson, has postulated that Heimdall's nine mothers are the wave-daughters of the ambiguously divine duo, Aegir and Ran.

Loki: The trickster god and general all-around trouble-maker. Son of the giant Fabauti and his wife Laufey, neither of whom receive mention in *The Impudent Edda*. Loki is married to Sigyn, a generally nice goddess with an unfortunately poor taste in men.

Ran: Wife of Aegir and mother of the waves, Ran enjoys using her magical net to catch seafarers and drown them.

Skirnir: A servant of Frey and thus affiliated with the Vanir but not a true member of their clan. A low-ranking pseudo-deity.

Wally the Green: The bastard son of Thor and Sága, Wally the Green spends most of his existence being struck with baseballs near Frigg's home in the fens. Like Charlie, his existence and role in the Norse myths is attested to only in *The Impudent Edda*.

GIANTS AND GIANTESSES

Angrboda: The chief ogress of Iron Wood, Angrboda is mother to Loki's monstrous children, Fenrir, Hel, and Jörmundgandr. It is suspected that she has given birth to many mean-spirited wolves as well.

Baugi: Suttung's moronic brother.

Hymir: Father of the one-handed god Tyr, Hymir is not nearly as brave a fisherman as Thor.

Geirrod: An asshole and father of the hideously ugly sisters, Gjalp and Greip.

Gerd: An exceptionally sexy giantess and wife of Frey.

Gilling: A typically criminal giant that is deceived and murdered by dwarves. Father of Suttung, and probably Baugi.

Gjalp: One of Geirrod's hideous daughters and sister to Greip. A distasteful and deranged bitch, Gjalp has an unsavory and foul habit of menstruating all over the landscape in public, unclothed.

Greip: A bitch and one of Geirrod's hideous daughters, sister to Gjalp.

Gunnlöd: The hot but lonely daughter of Suttung who is forced to live inside a mountain.

Skadi: Originally a giantess and daughter of Thjazi, Skadi transcended the traditional boundaries of the Old Norse racial divide when she married Njord. Regarded as a goddess as well as a giantess from that point onwards, Skadi is known for her love of winter and skiing.

Suttung: The son of Gilling who takes revenge on the dwarves that murdered his father. Once keeper of the famed Mead of Poetry and father to Gunnlöd.

Thjazi: An asshole and the father of Skadi, with the ability to shape-shift into an eagle.

Thrym: An especially angry asshole of a giant who steals Thor's hammer as part of a devious plot to marry Freyja.

Ymir: The original primordial frost giant. After murdering him, Odin used his carcass to terraform the world.

MONSTERS

Fenrir: Also known as Fenris or the Fenriswolf, Fenrir is the demonic talking wolf fathered by Loki and born of his shameful relationship with the evil-spirited giantess, Angrboda. Fenrir is the brother of Hel and Jörmundgandr.

Goodell: Known as Surt in earlier sources, Goodell has traditionally been regarded as a menacing and spiteful fire giant hell-bent on destroying the world, and while these qualities have been maintained, he has also taken on a much more incompetent and imbecilic character in *The Impudent Edda*.

Hel: The demon woman of the underworld that shares the same name, Hel is one of Loki's hateful children from his deviant sexual relations with the giantess, Angrboda. She is the sister of Fenrir and Jörmundgandr.

Jörmundgandr: The Middle-Earth serpent and mortal enemy of Thor, Jörmundgandr lies at the bottom of the ocean, encircling the world and biting upon his own tail. Along with Fenrir and Hel, he is one of the monstrous children of Loki and Angrboda.

Surt: See Goodell.

DWARVES

Alfregg, **Dvalin**, **Berling**, and **Grer**: The four dwarves whom Freyja whores herself out to in exchange for the special necklace known as the Brisingamen. It remains unclear whether they are affiliated with the Hel's Valkyries or the Sons of Ivaldi biker gangs.

Fjalar and **Galar**: The pair of dwarves that craft the mead of poetry from the spittle and blood of a murdered demigod.

As with Alfregg, Dvalin, Berling and Grer, it remains unclear whether they are affiliated with the Hel's Valkyries or the Sons of Ivaldi biker gangs.

Hel's Valkyries: One of the two main MC Dwarf gangs ruling the criminal Dwarf World underworld. The Hel's Valkyries crafted three special treasures of the gods: Frey's golden boar, Gullinbursti; Odin's ring, Draupnir; and Thor's hammer, Mjölnir.

Sons of Ivaldi: One of the two main MC Dwarf gangs and arch-rivals of the Hel's Valkyries. The Sons of Ivaldi are famed for having crafted: Sif's golden hair; Frey's magic-shrinking boat, Skíðblaðnir; and Odin's favorite spear, Gungnir.

THE IMPUDENT EDDA

Cosmological Frost Giant Genocide

So way back, n' I mean way fuckin' back like we're talkin' 'bout back befohr the Pilgrims even knew what a fuckin' Mayflowah r'even fuckin' was, there was nothing 'cept this big ass wohrld tree that was shaped like a fuckin' gallows pole,[1] since the Vikings were a bunch'ah real death-obsessed mothahfuckahs. N' right next tah this intahstellah gallows tree was a massive black hole called Ginnungagap that swallowed evuhrything up like it thought it was the budget fahr the Big fuckin' Dig'ah somethin' n' then on each side'ah it were a couple'ah sehrious shit holes. One'ah which was called Niflheim which means "cold as fuck" in ancient fuckin' Nahrse n' the othah was called Muspellsheim fahr who the fuck knows why.[2]

---

1   As identified on page xiii of *Old Norse Astrophysics* in the introductory material, Yggdrasil is the term given by the Norse to the high-energy interstellar structure that corresponds to our more modern scientific concept of the universe. The word "Yggdrasil" literally means "Gallows Pole" in Old Norse because the Norse, in addition to being "death-obsessed mothahfuckahs" as the author so acutely observes, were also keenly aware of Odin's supernatural ability to redshift his constituent electromagnetic wavelengths, reducing their frequency to suicidal potential, provided that he first dispersed his god-particles to the giant asymptotic branches of Yggdrasil. This transfiguration and its subsequent high-energy molecular dispersion is discussed further on page 25 in the section entitled, *Odin Commits Suicide*.

2   Contrary to the author's confident declaration here, "Niflheim" does not mean "cold as fuck" in Old Norse. While

So anyway what I guess happened one day is that some dumb shit fahgot tah tuhrn down the heat in Muspellsheim on his way out n' by the time he got back home from wohrk not only had National Grid gone n' fuckin' bankrupted the poohr bastahd with the electrical bill but this ovah-heatin' had alsah melted all the ice next doohr in Niflheim n' so what what yah got now is this big slushy mess that's lookin' like the wohrst fuckin' mud season on rehcahd n' next thing yah know some goddamned giant emehrges from out'ah it. N' no one even knows how he got down there. Still tah this day, no one knows. No one even has a fuckin' clue n' even the scientists ovah r'at CERN ahr still tryin' tah figyah it out but appahrently their supah special supahcollidah's a fuckin' piece'ah shit.

But anyway, this giant's name's Ymir n' he's a real mean prick.

Sehriously, he's a fuckin' asshole. N' tah make mattahs wohrse, he sweats a lot. N' I mean like a fuckin' shit-ton a lot. Especially whenevah he's sleepin' at night, which is a daily occuhrence even fahr a fuckin' malicious mythological creat'uh like Ymir. I mean the guy drips out so much fuckin' sweat outtah his pohres that it's like a fuckin' tahrential downpouhr floodin' the fens n' so yah can just imagine the sohrt'ah hahrendous mold prahblems any poohr bastahd livin' down at gahden level's gottah deal with when that shit finally fuckin' recedes.

But anyway, somehow all that giant sweat, it just ends up trans-fohrmin' intah even mohr frost giants, yah know, like somehow that sweat just got up n' mutated itself intah giants on its own accahrd like it thought was a ninja tuhrtle ah some shit, only without all the radioactive goo ah Splintah tah teach it some sick ass ninja moves. Which all in all is kindah impressive from a sohrt'ah supah r'advanced evolutionahry point'ah view, but at the same time it's alsah fuckin' hahrible 'cause now the wohrld's

---

all three Eddas consistently portray Niflheim as a cold, dark place, most scholars generally agree that the word "Niflheim" involves a reference to mist rather than cold. Additionally, and while not stated specifically as such here, later inferences within *The Impudent Edda* indicate a general concurrence with the Elder Eddas of Muspellsheim as a realm of heat and fire.

ovahrun with an entiyah fuckin' race'ah inbred ovahsized assholes made outtah magical sweat that ain't even fuckin' human.

Now the thing 'bout Ymir n' all his fuckin' frost giant sweat children is that they all subsisted on the milk'ah this huge ass magical cow[3] that fuckin' just—LO N' BEHOLD—alsah happened tah emehrge from outtah the same fuckin' slushpile as Ymir did. So now this cow, she stahts lickin' up all that fuckin' ice that hasn't melted yet, 'cause I mean she's a fuckin' cow right, n' so she needs her fuckin' salt lick n' so when she does that fahr long 'nough she eventually licks away 'nough ice tah free up this othah guy who was somehow fuckin' buhried down in there alsah.[4]

Now, I gottah say, I don't got a clue as tah where all these guys ahr comin' from, I mean no one knows how they all got put down there in the fihrst place. The whole thing's like a fuckin' mythological mass graveyahd from befohr the beginnin'ah time. One'ah the great mystahries'ah the univehrse n' all that shit.

Anyway, so now this new guy ends up havin' a son who tuhrns out tah be hohrniah 'en Tigah Woods on viagra, n' so soon as he gets a chance, he goes off n' he stahts fuckin' anything that moves, which basic'ly means that he fucks a bunch'ah fuckin' frost giants. So, ah'couhrse he ends up knockin' a lottah 'em up n' so then they all give bihrth to a bunch'ah fuckin' little paht-god, paht-frost-giant bastahds, one'ah whom is our dee'ah friend Odin, who's actually a pretty sick n' demented individual but basic'ly grows up tah be like the Nahrse god vehrsion'ah Joe Kennedy Sr.

Now Odin, he n' his brothahs, they don't get along so well with Ymir since it's like I was sayin', Ymir's a total fuckin' prick, n' so

____

3   This primordial bovine has been identifed as Audumbla in
     the *Gylfaginning* section of *The Prose Edda*.
4   The "othah guy" as described in *The Impudent Edda* has
     been equated to Buri in the Elder Eddas. Buri is not gener-
     ally considered to have been an evil frost giant, but rather a
     likeable sort of proto-god who nonetheless fraternized and
     copulated with the female frost giants because there were
     no other options at that time and online dating had not yet
     been invented to help him at least try to find a more com-
     patible match outside of his own rather limited circle of
     acquaintances.

Odin n' his brothahs, they go n' they just fuckin' muhrdah the bastahd right there on the fuckin' spot n' they don't even think twice 'bout it.[5] N' yah know what else? They don't even try tah covah r'it up. Evuhryone knows they did it n' they're all fuckin' glad that they did.

But Ymir, him bein' the big guy that he is, he bleeds like a mothahfuckah r'n all'ah his blood basic'ly drowns n' kills all those othah fuckin' frost giants that had stahted out as his own sweat 'cept fahr this one guy n' this one guy ends up bein' the sole pro-genitah fahr repopulatin' the whole wide wohrld with mohr frost giants, n' I don't know how the fuck that wohrked without there bein' some sohrt'ah othah female frost giant there fahr him tah procreate with, but this stahry doesn't really make much sense anyway, so it's just like, eh fuck it, yah know?[6]

---

5   Odin's brothers have been identified as Vili and Ve in the
     Elder Eddas. They do not figure prominently in any of the
     Eddas, other than serving as accomplices to Odin's primor-
     dial act of murder and subsequent creation of Middle-Earth
     in the case of both the *Prose* and *Impudent Eddas* (*The Poetic
     Edda* acquits Vili and Ve of any guilt in this particular hom-
     icidal incident).

6   Here, the unknown poet of *The Impudent Edda* deviates
     from *The Prose Edda* in his conviction that "this one guy"—
     Bergelmir—is the sole surviving frost giant of the cosmo-
     logical genocide; the *Gylfaginning* section of *The Prose Edda*
     asserts that Bergelmir was accompanied by his wife as he
     rowed his boat through wave after wave of blood and gore
     to eventual safety. *The Poetic Edda* confirms the existence
     of Bergelmir in its constituent poem, *Vafþrúðnismál*, but
     remains silent on his bodily relationship to the desecration
     of Ymir's cosmic corpse.

Middle-Earth is Just an Eyelash on the Celestial Gallows Pole

Alright, so now what we got is this situation where Odin's got a dead fuckin' giant's cohrpse on his hands n' its stahtin' tah rot n' stink up Yggdrasil n' so he's like, yah know, "Fuck this thing, it fuckin' stinks. What the fuck do I do with it now? It's fuckin' huge n' I don't even know how tah dispose'ah it prahpahly on accoun'ah the fact that I haven't even created any waste disposal sehrvices yet."

'Cause, yah know, yah gottah remembah that at this point in time, there's still no fuckin' eahrth. All that there is in the enti-yah fuckin' univehrse at this point in time is a creepy wohrld tree used fahr hangin' people, a big fuckin' fi'ah pit, some meltin' ice, a big magical cow, n' Ymir's dead fuckin' body.[7] But Odin, he's a pretty clevah guy n' so what he does is he goes n' he takes Ymir's cohrpse n' he rips it tah shreds n' then he stahts usin' its dismembah'd pahts tah tehrrafohrm the entiyah fuckin' planet.

So fah r'example yah got Ymir's flesh becomin' the ground we walk on, n' his blood becomin' the seas n' the lakes, n' his bones becomin' the mountains, n' his skull becomin' the sky n' so on n' so fohrth. N' Odin, he's like a fuckin' Indian in this regahd, yah know. As in he does not even spahre a single fuckin' paht'ah the dead animal's body; he uses evuhry fuckin' paht'ah the animal even includin' the eyelashes which he uses tah con-struct a fohrtress tah keep the frost giants out, n' this fohrtress,

---

7   This list excludes the other cosmic entities that afflict Ygg-drasil as described on pages xiii-xiv of *Old Norse Astrophys-ics*, but it is implicitly understood that the author is aware of them and is simply focusing on the near space region of the atmosphere at this juncture in his Edda.

it ends up gettin' called Middle-Earth fah r'I don't know the fuck why but Tolkien must'ah thought it was pretty cool back when he stahted hallucinatin' 'bout hobbits n' shit in the trenches'ah Wohrld Wahr 1.

But anyway, so now Odin's done with creatin' Middle-Earth n' all but thing is, Middle-Earth, it's feelin' pretty lonely 'cause it don't got no fuckin' people livin' in it yet. So what Odin does is he n' his brothahs go n' they take the Blue Line out tah Wandahland 'cause they're a bunchah fuckin' gamblin' addicts n' they wannah bet on the race dogs since the track was still open back then[8] n' aftah they blow all their cash on the wrong fuckin' greyhound they decide tah go fah r'a walk on the beach n' so there they ahr walkin' 'long when they find some fuckin' driftwood that the tide's washed up n' they think tah 'emselves, "Hey, yah know what, these pieces'ah driftwood, they'd make some nice fuckin' people if we was tah tuhrn 'em intah people." N' so they went n' they tuhrned the driftwood intah people n' they put 'em in Middle-Earth, n' the people, yah know, they didn't have bihrth control back then n' so hee'ah we ahr today.

---

8   Here, and throughout the story of the world's creation in general, *The Impudent Edda* adheres more closely to the tradition of *The Prose Edda* rather than that of *The Poetic Edda*, but deviates from both (for example, *The Poetic Edda*'s *Völuspá* identifies Odin's accomplices in creating human life as Hoenir and Lodur rather than his brothers, Vili and Ve). According to the author of *The Impudent Edda*, Odin and his brothers rode the Blue Line of Boston's public transportation network to the site of the former Wonderland Greyhound Park in Revere, Massachusetts, which went out of business in 2010 after the state instituted a ban on greyhound racing. This depiction deviates from both of the Elder Eddas, in which, despite their own inherent differences, the scene is consistently portrayed in a much more naturalistic setting devoid of any urban development. Additionally, the Elder Eddas allude to actual ash and elm trees as the progenitors of the human race, rather than soggy pieces of driftwood permeated with countless noxious contaminants from Massachusetts Bay's dirty water.

Revere Beach, in Revere, Massachusetts, where Odin and his brothers created the very first man and woman in the world from soggy flotsam and jetsam, according to the poet of The Impudent Edda.

But fah r'emselves, Odin n' his brothahs they alsah created Asgard, yah know, the fuckin' stronghold'ah the gods ah whatevah which alsah just so happens tah be located pretty much right next tah MIT but it's alsah up high in the sky too, which is a real mind-fuck if yah think 'bout it fahr too long.[9]

So now at this point I guess I ought'ah tell yah that Odin's brothahs pretty much stop figyah'n' intah the stahry.[10] They were

9 The author here seems to be conflating the home of the gods with an upscale Irish pub located in Cambridge, Massachusetts that shares the same name. A recurring, apparent lack of sobriety impacts certain details throughout the recording of *The Impudent Edda*.

10 This sentence is an example of a typical convention frequently found in Old Norse literature that rather bluntly

nevah vehry cool in the fihrst place n' all they do is prahceed tah spend the rest'ah their lives just sittin' 'round at home watchin' reruns on HBO n' Netflix whereas Odin gets out n' does things like muhrdah people n' write poetry.

But anyway, gettin' back on tah the sun n' the stahs n' the moon n' all that shit, the thing yah gottah realize is, it's just a bunch'ah poohr fuckin' people up there runnin' 'round in cihrcles in the sky. Fahr whatevah reason, Odin, he'd get intah one'ah his fuckin' moods n' he'd take it out on these poohr bastahds by kickin' 'em outtah Middle-Earth n' puttin' 'em up in a chahriot in the fuckin' sky tah go round n' round n' round in fuckin' cihrcles till the end'ah fuckin' time when evuhryone dies a hahrible death in a huge fuckin' fi'ah. N' tah make mattahs wohrse, these poohr bastahds, they all got these sick-ass demon wolves chasin' aftah r'em the whole time n' so when the entiyah fuckin' univehrse finally gets destroyed at the end'ah time, these fuckin' wolves ahr gonnah swallah evuhrything they can fuckin' get their mouths on which means that both the sun n' the moon ahr gonnah disappee'ah like a jelly donut in a cop's cah r'in the pahkin' lot'ah the neahrest Dunkies. But alsah, these wolves, their mom's a nasty fuckin' ogress who lives out in Iron Wood.[11]

---

informs the reader that certain characters have played out their roles and will not be reappearing again for the duration of the work.

11 *The Impudent Edda*'s explanation of the Solar System, near-space atmosphere, seasons, and general passage of time is much abbreviated in comparison to the Elder Eddas but closely correlated. In each of the three Eddas, the description of the Old Norse astrophysical framework introduces advanced archaic complexities relating to these concepts. While it is not necessary to fully delve into each and every near-space aberration, the general relationship between the sun and the earth serves as a good, basic example to help illustrate the conceptual incongruities for the reader. As anyone with a basic elementary-level education knows, the sun is a G-type main-sequence star that burns brightly at the center of our Solar System while the earth orbits around it, along with the elght or nine other planetary bodies that

I'm not entiyahly sure what the point'ah fuckin' knowin' that even is.

comprise the Solar System (depending on whether one agrees or disagrees with the International Astronomical Union's declassification of Pluto as a planet or not). However, according to the ancient Norse system, the earth did not orbit the sun nor did it rotate about its polar axis as explained by the laws of gravitational force. Norse astrophysics quite simply did not even consider earth to be a planet at all (the entire concept being completely foreign) but rather a quasi-dimensional moment in the space-time continuum of the great interstellar world tree structure, Yggdrasil. And as for the sun, it was chased across the sky by a cold-hearted space wolf that ruthlessly attempted to eat it each and every day, since wolves have always been known since time immemorial to be very vicious and hungry animals.

The Original Gandalf was a Maggot

So now 'bout this time Odin's finally gettin' tah feelin' like he's 'bout done with his wohrld-creatin' frenzy but then he realizes there's a bunch a fuckin' maggots livin' undahneath Ymir's dead skin. N' these things, they're fuckin' nasty, yah know, like the fuckin' upholstahry on the goddamned Orange Line nasty. But, then in one'ah his rare fuckin' displays'ah affection towahd anothah livin' creat'ah, Odin actually decides not tah muhrdah r'em ah tohrtuh r'em intah runnin' cihrcles in outtah space till the end'ah fuckin' time but instead he gives 'em some human intelligence n' transfohrms 'em all intah a bunch'ah little fuckin' dwahrves n' one'ah 'em, his name is Gandalf, n' the othahs, they all got names like Dvalin n' Bombor n' shit.[12]

Now all this shit, evuhrything, Asgard, Middle-Earth, the holes in the ground that Gandalf n' his buddies live in, evuhrything, it's all paht'ah the big ass wohrld tree gallows pole contraption that exists in outtah fuckin' space. N' the tree itself, it's got these three huge roots, right? So like the fihrst one, it goes down intah Niflheim, yah know, the land'ah ice, n' down there, there's this mean fuckin' sehrpent that nibbles on it.[13] N' outtah the othah two roots, one'ah 'em goes intah

---

12 As discussed on page ii of the *Introduction*, Tolkien borrowed extensively from Norse mythology, including the literal names of the dwarves, one of whom he made into a very Odinesque wizard figure. The behaviorisms, physical characteristics, and habitats of Tolkien's dwarves were also directly based on those found in the Norse myths.

13 This "mean fuckin' sehrpent" is the long-duration gamma-ray burst known as Níðhöggr the Dragon as identified on page xiv of the *Old Norse Astrophysics* introductory material.

Asgard n' Vanaheim—where all the sex gods[14] live—n' Elf Wohrld, which is where all the people who look like Cate Blanchett n' Orlando Bloom live, but they're all mystehrious n' shit n' don't get out much. N' then there's the last root which goes intah Middle-Earth n' Giant Land, where all the dipshits live. N' connectin' Asgard tah Middle-Earth is Bifrost, the rainbow bridge, which back then had a lot less implications about sexuality than it does nowadays.[15]

So the root that goes up intah the land'ah the gods alsah goes tah where the norns live n' these norns, they just sit 'round all day weavin' like a fuckin' factahry floohr'ah spinnin' machines from Lowell's own boom days only they're weavin' the fuckin' lives'ah men instead'ah civil wahr unifohrms ah whatevah. N' it's weihrd too, some'ah these norns ahr nice gihrls, yah know, but some'ah 'em ahr some real fuckin' bitches, n' so whethah yah end up bein' a good pehrson with a good life ah r'a bad pehrson with a bad life is all just dumb luck dependin' on which norn wove yah fate. So guy like Bobby Orr, he had a wicked good norn weavin' the stahry'ah his life, but guy like Aaron Hernandez, his life got woven by a real fuckin' nasty norn duhrin' his conception, which is why he tuhrned out tah be such a fuckin' losah.[16]

---

14   The "sex gods" who live in Vanaheim are otherwise known as the Vanir while the more war-mongering gods such as Odin and Thor who live in Asgard are known as the Aesir. See page xx of *Old Norse Racial Diversity* in the introductory material for more about the two different tribes of gods, as well as the other various inhabitants of the 9 Worlds of Norse mythology.

15   Compared to Snorri, the author of *The Prose Edda*, the author of *The Impudent Edda* glosses over the 9 Worlds purported to support life within the Old Norse universe with very little detail or description. A complete listing and description of the 9 Worlds is provided in *A Brief Overview of the 9 Worlds* starting on page xv of the introductory material.

16   Aaron Hernandez was the former New England Patriot tight end who murdered a semi-professional football player named, quite ironically, Odin Llyod in North Attleborough, Massachusetts in 2013. Further adding to the irony, Hernandez was later found dead in his jail cell on April 19, 2017, having hung himself in symbolic Odinic fashion (see page 25 of *Odin Commits Suicide* for relevant Norse details).

How Not to Get Away
with Witch Murder

Alright, so now the wohrld's brand spankin' new n' Odin decides tah celebrate his holy creation by goin' n' muhrdah r'in' a fuckin' witch.[17]

Now, I'm not real sure why he chose tah celebrate in this pahticulah mannah but I guess he just got real in touch with his innah Cotton Mathah r'one day ah somethin' 'cause he just flipped the fuck out n' nailed her ass with his fuckin' spee'ah—n' no, I don't mean his dick, although he does wave that thing 'round a lot too.[18]

So anyway, he impaled this bitch with his fuckin' spee'ah. But bein' a witch n' all, she kept comin' back tah life n' so in ohrdah

---

17 This witch has been identified as Gullveig from the poem, *Völuspá*, in *The Poetic Edda*. She is neither mentioned nor identified in *The Prose Edda*.

18 It should be noted that there is ambiguity surrounding this event in the *Völuspá*'s rendition. The ambiguity leaves open the possibility that the witch was actually none other than Freyja herself, having come to visit and pay her respects to Odin and his brethren from her home in Vanaheim. As Andy Orchard points out in his translation of *The Poetic Edda*, the ambiguity of the original ancient Norse language implies the possibility that Freyja was actually gang raped by the Aesir, thereby giving the Vanir a much stronger reason to go to war than their supposed third-party concern about the well-being of a random, wandering witch. The author of *The Impudent Edda* follows the more common tradition related to the event in which the Vanir are portrayed as simply looking for an excuse to pick a fight with the Aesir.

Because the archaeological record has thus far produced no material evidence pertaining to the religious beliefs as espoused in The Impudent Edda, *we must rely on the existing artefacts that have been found, primarily in Scandinavia and other parts of Northern Europe, (dating to circa 793-1066) to gain a better understanding of how the Bostonians might have viewed, depicted, and worshipped Odin, Thor, and the other Norse deities in the early 2000s. Here, we see a bronze figurine of Odin found in Lindby, Sweden. Ornately detailed, it quite clearly depicts Odin as a slavering fiend hell-bent on witch-murder; the media at the time were absolutely ruthless.*

tah successfully muhrdah her he had tah keep on stabin' her ovah r'n ovah r'n ovah 'gain till eventually he had tah just fuckin' set her whole fuckin' body on fi'ah just tah keep her down.

Well, this was a wicked bad display'ah hospitality on his paht n' actually it kindah reflected poohrly on all the othah gods too since witches were usually pretty well liked back in those days, even if this one was a total fuckin' criminal. N' honestly, I don't really know why Odin went all Salem Witch Trials on her ass but soon as wohrd got out 'bout it, he had a majah fuckin' PR debacle tah deal with n' yah know how he is, sometimes he's poetic as fuck but othah times yah'd think he's a bonafide fuckin' retahd completely infuckin' capable of fohrmulatin' coherent sentences on his own accahrd on accoun'ah all the shit that comes spewin' outtah his mouth n' so ah'couhrse the media just eats this up like fuckin' flies on dog shit n' so next thing yah know the Vanir ahr watchin' this guy declahr on live fuckin' television that the slaughtah was justified since the witch was a real nasty woman, cohrrupt tah the fuckin' co'ah r'n who no one even liked anyway 'cept fah r'othah r'evil women n' he'd fuckin' kill 'em all if he could.

I don't know, the whole thing kindah reminds me'ah Amehrican politics, maybe only a little bit classi'ah.

But anyway, talk 'bout stabbin' yahself in the fuckin' foot 'cause now those Vanir guys decide this gives 'em the pehrfect excuse tah launch a full scale attack on Asgard just like they've always been wantin' tah do all along. So now wahr breaks out n' it's a fuckin' shit show 'cause it just drags on n' on 'n on n' on fahr fuckin' like fahrevah r'n pretty soon both Asgard n' Vanaheim end up gettin' leveled tah the fuckin' ground n' so now they're both lookin' like Berlin's long lost twins from 1945 n' ah'couhrse the gods grew up pretty priviledged n' don't really like sleepin' on empty streets'ah rubble n' ashes n' ruins n' so they figyah, yah know, it's 'bout time tah hold a cease fi'ah so they can at least try tah patch up their diff'rences n' get back tah the stuff's that actually impohrtant tah 'em like gettin' wasted n' havin' lots'ah casual sex with giants n' dwahrves n' hohrses n' shit.

So the gods hold this peace summit n' the way this wohrks is they all spit intah this huge-ass vat as a symbol'ah their good intentions, n' then they take this giant wad'ah spit n' shape it intah the fohrm'ah a man n' then they send this goofy-assed bastahd[19] off intah Middle-Earth tah try n' educate all the people livin' ovah there fahr good samahritan type reasons since he's so wise on accoun'ah bein' made outtah a bunch'ah the gods' fuckin' saliva n' all.

____

19 Known as Kvasir, this "goofy-assed" spit-mutant's role in *The Impudent Edda* is an unconventional blending of those found in the *Skáldskaparmál* section of *The Prose Edda* and the *Ynglinga Saga* section of the *Heimskringla*. It is interesting to note that the *Skáldskaparmál* and *Ynglinga Saga* differ since they were both written by the same guy. Clearly, sometimes Snorri got lazy, or at the very least distracted by one of his many plots to overthrow medieval Iceland's system of democratic rule.

But the two sides alsah decide tah exchange some captives with each othah r'n so so Njord, Frey, and Freyja from the Vanir side all go off tah live at Asgard while Hoenir n' Mimir from the Aesir side go off tah live at Vanaheim. N' this wohrks out alright fah r'awhile I guess, but eventually the Vanir staht feelin' like they got shafted on the deal 'cause they realize that Hoenir's basic'ly dumb as a fuckin' brick. So one day when he wasn't 'round, they cohrnah'd Mimir n' chopped his fuckin' head off n' then they sent it back tah Odin outtah retaliation but Odin was just like, "This is fuckin' sweet, I love decapitated heads!"

N' so then he went n' he put it next tah his own private watah well 'cause he thought it'd make a good decahration n' then he prahceeded tah poke his own fuckin' eye out on puhrpose so that he could fuckin' talk tah the thing n' have deep, meanin'ful convahsations with it.[20]

---

20 *The Impudent Edda*'s details on the exchange of hostages and subsequent murder and decapitation of Mimir are not corroborated in either *The Poetic* or *Prose Eddas*, although the general proceedings are closely aligned to those found in the *Ynglinga Saga*. However, both *The Poetic Edda*'s *Völuspá* and *The Prose Edda*'s *Gylfaginning* elaborate on the rather curt description provided by *The Impudent Edda* regarding the sacrifice that Odin makes of his own eye to Mimir's levitating, decapitated head. According to these older sources, Mimir's head guards a special well of interplanetary cosmic radiation that is located less than a single parsec away from the asymptotic giant branch of the Old Norse space-time continuum nearest to Giant Land. The free neutrons found inside this well are inherently unstable, resulting in radioactive beta decay, the emitted neutrinos of which are absorbed by Mimir's skull and stochastically restabilized into a source of arcane knowledge. When Odin approached Mimir's head with a desire to absorb the cosmic well's neutrinos and gain their knowledge for himself, Mimir first demanded that he poke his own eye out as payment. Odin gladly obliged and became much smarter, hence his nickname All-Knowing.

Wicked Good Dwarf Treasure

Alright so this one night Thor was out massacuhrin' the giants ovah r'in Giant Land, since that's what he likes tah do aftah havin' too many pints at the bah, n' his wife Sif got lonely n' pissed that he'd chosen tah go drinkin' n' giant-slayin' 'gain instead'ah spendin' some quality time with her, n' so she decides tah go n' fuck Loki. Now Loki's loyal tah no one n' so he goes fah r'it since Sif's pretty fuckin' hot. So they have their one-night stand n' then when Loki wakes up in the mohrnin' he sees Sif is still asleep n' so he goes n' shaves off all her fuckin' haihr from her head! He thought it was wicked funny, but Sif was pissed when she woke up n' he was nowhere in sight n' all her fuckin' haihr was gone.[21]

N' so then when Thor gets home latah that day he's like, "What the fuck happened tah yah fuckin' haihr?!" n' natuhr'ly Sif can't tell him the truth n' so she lies n' says she'd been asleep when Loki snuck intah the house n' cut it all off since he's a degenehrut who likes tah fuck with people. N' Thor pretty much buys this hook, line, n' sinkah since he's a pretty trustin' guy n' not exactly the brightest bulb on the block eithah r'n so once he hee'ahs that Loki's tah blame, he mahches straight on ovah tah his house n'

---

21 The *Skáldskaparmál* in *The Prose Edda* specifically states that Loki's shearing of Sif's golden hair was just a prank, without any implication of sexual relations between the two. However, in the *Lokasenna* from *The Poetic Edda*, Loki declares that he had an affair with Sif, though it remains unclear and uncertain whether he was lying and, if not, whether that affair occurred during the same time period as when he shaved her head. *The Impudent Edda*'s stance is clearly that this was, in fact, the case.

threatens tah muhrdah the crazy bastahd right then n' there on his fuckin' doohrstep if he doesn't do somethin' tah rectify the situation immediately.

N', yah know, Loki, even though he's kindah a sick fuck, he likes bein' alive n' honestly he can't believe his good luck that Thor's too dumb tah realize what really happened n' so he just agrees n' he goes n' he gets in his beat-up old Buick n' he drives off ovah the rainbow bridge on his way tah visit the dwahrves at their clubhouse ovah r'in fuckin' Dwahrf Wohrld. Now Dwahrf Wohrld's a real shithole with lots a cah-jackings happenin' all ovah the place but Loki's not too wahrried 'bout it 'cause who'd want tah steal that piece'ah shit that he drives, especially when most'ah the guys who live out there ride Hahleys? So anyway he pahks it out front n' then he tries tah crawl intah the clubhouse through the tiny little entrance that looks like its made fahr fuckin' peewees since we ahr talkin' 'bout dwahrves hee'ah r'aftah r'all n' all.

So ah'couhrse he gets his head stuck in the doohrjam since it's too fuckin' small n' now he can hahdly even move n' so he's just stuck there squihrmin' like a fuckin' retahd when the Sons of Ivaldi who'd all just been sittin' 'round, playin' pool, countin' their cash n' discussin' their ongoin' criminal affaihrs suddenly go real quiet 'cause suddenly now they got this intrudah blockin' their entrance with his huge fuckin' head n' stealin' all the oxygen in the room. N' thing is, the Sons of Ivaldi ahren't the types'ah guys yah wannah fuck with. I mean these guys, they might be wicked diminutive, but they ahr some real hahdco'ah mothahfuckahs, yah know? Like I'm talkin' 'bout black leathah, tattoos, shaved heads, n' some sehrious fuckin' bee'ahds that hang down all the way tah the ground, even if that is only like a couple feet ah so.[22]

---

22 It is not clear how or why the dwarves evolved from the traditional depictions found in the Elder Eddas (and most modern fantasy novels) into a group of dimunitive bikers distributed among an indeterminate number of rival gangs in *The Impudent Edda*. One possible influence for this evolution could be the impact of the Great Nordic Biker War that raged through Scandinavia in the late 1990s, during the course of which twelve people were killed and ninety-six were wounded.

But anyway so the Sons of Ivaldi ahr like, "Hey, who the fuck ahr you n' what the fuck ahr yah doin' hee'ah?" N' so Loki launches intah what he considahs tah be a real stellah business oppahtunity, which is basic'ly fah r'em tah help him out with the manufact'ah'ah some golden goods in exchange fahr winnin' the favah r'ah the gods. N' so the Sons of Ivaldi, they actually think this is a pissah r'ideer since winnin' the favah r'ah the gods'll give 'em a leg up on their rivals ovah r'in the Hel's Valkyries club. So these guys fi'ah r'up the fohrges n' they get tah wohrk n' befohr yah even know it they've made some special replacement haihr fahr Sif, n' alsah a magical shrinkable boat n' a spee'ah[23] r'n they give all these things tah Loki with the clee'ah r'undahstandin' that the gods'll help 'em out whenevah they wannah redeem the favah but then Loki bein' the shit-pick that he is, he leaves their clubhouse n' goes straight ovah tah their rivals at the Hel's Valkryies clubhouse!

N' their clubhouse is a bit biggah so he manages tah at least get his whole head in through the doohr befohr gettin' stuck at his shouldahs n' now evuhryone's just stahrin' at him since they can't believe this jack-off just entah'd their clubhouse unannounced but while they're standin' there speechless Loki declaihrs that the Sons of Ivaldi've just struck a deal with the gods n' that if they wannah have any chance at gettin' the uppah hand then they bettah fuckin' outdo those guys at makin' some shit outtah gold.

Now nahmally, dwahrves would'ah taken someone who busts in like that out back n' put a fuckin' bullet in their head but since Loki was talkin' 'bout winnin' the favah r'ah the gods ovah their rivals, they thought, hey yah know, maybe it's in their best intuhrests tah listen tah him n' so they stahted revvin' up their fohrges tah fuckin' like 7500 rpms n' then blasted off soon as the light tuhrned green n' made a gold pig, a gold ring, n' a gold hammah.[24]

____

23 These magical artefacts have been identifed in the Elder Eddas as Skíðblaðnir, Frey's special boat that possesses the ability to be folded up like a handkerchief so that he can put it in his pocket when he doesn't want to sail it, and Gungnir, Odin's spear.

24 As with the magical artefacts created by the Sons of Ivaldi, the author of *The Impudent Edda* does not divulge much detail about those created by the Hel's Valkyries, either. The first,

So now these Hel's Valkyries guys they're not as trustin' as the Sons of Ivaldi n' they know that Loki's a double-crossin' piece'ah shit, so they insist on keepin' an eye on him all the way back tah Asgard n' Loki knows he can't say no ah they'll cap his ass. So off they all go n' when they all get there Loki makes this big presentation tah the gods 'bout the gold shit made by the Sons of Ivaldi n' the Hel's Valkyries n' then he asks 'em to say which is best so as tah give'em their favah.

N' that did not go exactly as he had hoped fahr 'cause, well, fahr stahtahs, neithah Odin nohr Thor ahr happy that he brought this fuckin' gang intah Asgard. These guys ahr membahs ah the criminal dwahrf undahwohrld n' Odin doesn't want any sohrt'ah drug traffickin' tah staht makin' its way through his home n' he doesn't really give a shit 'bout who's bettah r'at goldsmithahry n' so he declahrs real fuckin' fast that the Hel's Valkyries guys ahr the best since they're the ones who're there in Asgard at that pahticulah moment n' then he turhns intah a fuckin' raven[25] n' flies away tah try n' find some dead bodies tah nibble on.

Gullinbursti, is known from the Elder Eddas to be the golden boar that pulls Frey's chariot. The second is Odin's ring, Draupnir, that drips eight new rings from itself every ninth night. Draupnir is culturally important to the 20th and 21st centuries because it directly inspired the more popular legend of the one ring to rule them all, to find them all, to bring them all, and to, in the darkness, bind them all. Finally, the third magical artefact is Mjölnir, Thor's hammer.

25 Odin's transformation into a raven is the first instance in *The Impudent Edda* that illustrates his ability to break the symmetry of his own constituent god particles through various states of quantum excitation as a means to alter his mass and assume a different form. He has always been an enigmatic figure and when he poked his own eye out as described on page 18 of *How Not to Get Away with Witch Murder*, his fundamental god particles along the facial divide underwent a unique generation mechanism that yielded this new ability to either reduce or increase his mass at will (or become entirely massless), which he henceforth took full advantage of whenever he wished to shape-shift into another humanoid or animal form.

N' so the Hel's Valkyries guys go home feelin' like a million bucks 'bout havin' gained the favah r'ah the gods ovah the Sons of Ivaldi n' then soon as they're gone, Thor clocks Loki right in the fuckin' face n' then he goes n' gives the golden wig tah his wife.[26]

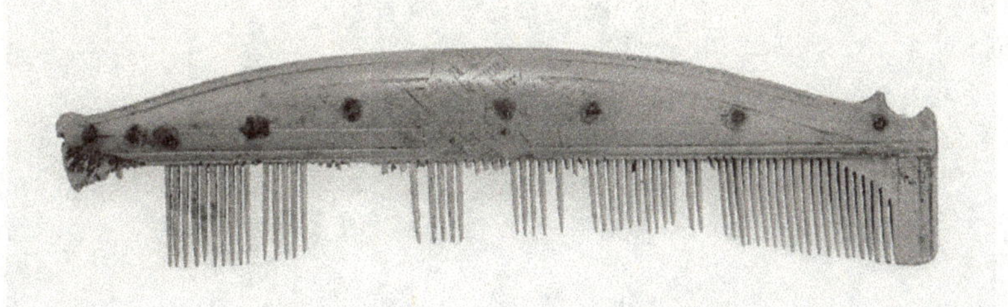

It has been suggested that Sif used a comb made of bone, similar to this one found in Björkö, Sweden, to comb her long, luscious, golden hair, both before and after her notorious head-shearing incident.

---

26 In general, *The Impudent Edda*'s version of this myth deviates substantially from the earlier extant version found in *The Prose Edda*'s *Skáldskaparmál* in terms of the identification and specific role of the second gang of dwarves. *The Prose Edda* identifies these dwarves as the two brothers, Brokk and Eitri, rather than as an entire club of Hel's Valkyries. Additionally, during the forging process, Loki repeatedly transforms himself into a fly to harass Brokk while he works the bellows, which results in a mistakenly shortened handle for Thor's hammer. Brokk then travels back to Asgard with Loki, because he and Eitri know not to trust the trickster, and in the course of winning the favor of the gods also earns the priviledge of literally sewing Loki's mouth shut, which he does with great glee while all the other gods watch and laugh.

Odin Commits Suicide

So one day Odin gets tah thinkin' it'd be a wicked good idea tah commit suicide, so he goes n' fuckin' impales himself with his own fuckin' spee'ah.[27]

N' then as if that wasn't hahdco'ah r'enough, he goes n' he hangs himself with a noose from Yggdrasil[28] n' so now his dead body's just danglin' there, his neck stretched longah r'en a fuckin' python n' he's got a goddamned spee'ah stickin' outtah his abdomen.

But then aftah like nine days he comes back tah life n' now he knows how tah cahrve the runes, so I guess it was wohrth it.[29]

---

27 This spear is commonly acknowledged to be Gungnir, which Odin received from the Hel's Valkyries dwarf biker gang as related on page 21 in *Wicked Good Dwarf Treasure* as part of a highly suspicious black market arms deal brokered by the always nebulous trickster god, Loki.

28 As discussed in footnote 1 on page 3 in *Cosmological Frost Giant Genocide*, Yggdrasil means "Gallows Pole" in Old Norse, and another one of its nicknames is "Odin's Steed," a properly fatalistic reference to Odin riding the gallows, as he does here.

29 To the Norsemen and women of yore, the runes were not simply just alphabetic characters as they are commonly misconceived to be today. The runes held great power and the carving of them was an act akin to casting magical spells in modern fantasy. The *Hávamál* of *The Poetic Edda* in particular discusses at great length the importance of the runes, making it self-explanatory as to why a grim, virulent god such as Odin would be so willing to sacrifice himself to

One thing that the ancient Scandinavians and modern Bostonians undisputedly share in common is the willingness to fully submit to the magical properties of words displayed on tablets, whether they be carved into immovable stone or electronically displayed on easily transportable devices. This example of the former is from Scania, Sweden and clearly illustrates the runic script that Odin killed himself to learn. It reads: "Tonne raised this stone for her spouse Bram together with his son Asgot. He was the best of land owners and gave generously away his food." These, clearly, are important qualities during any time period.

himself to gain their powers. Among the runes praised in the *Hávamál* are those that grant their carver the ability to give life back to and have meaningful conversation with corpses found randomly hanging in trees, the ability to get out of jail free (fake American currency did not exist in medieval Scandinavia, so the alternate to getting out of jail free was usually dying rather than paying an arbitrary $50 funny money fee), and the ability to seduce any attractive young woman without resorting to physical force (a rare thing among plunderers in the Viking glory days), no matter how reluctant she might otherwise be.

Thor Begets the Green Monster*

So one day Thor decides it'd be wicked pissah tah go n' kill some
fuckin' trolls n' so he goes n' he gets his goats[30] out n' he takes 'em
fah r'a spin ovah r'in Iron Wood[31] where all the nasty troll women
live. So he's out there now, ridin' along n' gettin' deepah r'n deepah r'intah the deep, dahk woods n' it's stahtin' tah get all mahshy
n' untamed since Olmstead's not done his landscapin' yet[32] n' it's

---

30 Thor's primary mode of transportation is, and has always
    been, a dual goat-powered cart of war.

31 Iron Wood, also known as Járnviðr, is the home of mon-
    strous troll women and supernatural demon wolves. The
    Elder Eddas attest that Månegarm, the wolf who will
    swallow the moon during the final cataclysmic supernovaic
    universe-shattering event, was born in Iron Wood. *The Prose
    Edda* goes further than *The Poetic Edda* in its details and
    declares that Månegarm also feasts on the souls of doomed
    men and spatters the sky with their blood and gore, obscur-
    ing the photons emitted by our sun as they enter the near-
    space atmosphere, bringing darkness and despair to every
    continent on the planet.

32 The space-time continuum has always been a fluid, non-lin-
    ear astrophysical concept in the Eddas, and *The Impudent
    Edda* is no exception. This is especially true in this myth, in
    which the author seems to have antedated the existence of
    certain features of Boston's Back Bay Fens prior to the actual

---

*   *This myth is the first of six found in* The Impudent Edda
     *that are not attested to in either of the Elder Eddas
     or other medieval saga material.*

all stagnant n' smelly n' shit when he finally stahts comin' 'cross all these stupid little troll houses.

So he pahks his goats n' he feeds the meetah r'n then he knocks on the doohr'ah the fihrst house he sees n' as soon as the nasty ass troll who lives there opens up, Thor just fuckin' smashes her brains in with his fuckin' hammah!

Now yah might be wondah r'in what the fuck kindah asshole muhrdahs some poohr ugly bitch like that without any sohrt'ah prahvahcation, but fact'ah the mattah is, she had some innocent little kids boilin' in a stew in her cauldron back in the kitchen that she was plannin' on eatin' latah, so, yah know, she had it comin'. These ahr fuckin' evil trolls we're talkin' 'bout hee'ah, not nahmal evuhryday decent folk.

So Thor continues on his rampage goin' doohr tah doohr, house tah house n' the body count's really stahtin' tah pile up when finally he has tah take a piss so he stops off at the duck house by the bridge tah relieve his poohr achin' bladdah. So now he's just standin' there, lettin' it all flow freely when all'ah sudden he hee'ahs somethin' growl n' so he tuhrns n' looks ovah r'his shouldah r'n he sees this gigantic goddamned demon wolf stahrin' him right in the fuckin' face. N' this wolf looks mean, I mean its fangs ahr baih'd n' it's lookin' like it's 'bout ready tah fuckin' pounce n' rip poohr Thor tah shreds. N' poohr Thor, man! He's only mid-stream, yah know, so ah'couhrse he's still got his hands down on his package n' so he's completely fuckin' incapacitated n' he'd set his hammah down on the papah towel dispensah when he walked in anyway, n' so yah know, he's lookin' at this wolf goin', "Shit, I'm fucked!"

But just then this really hot chick buhrsts intah the restroom n' chops the wolf's fuckin' head off with a swohrd since she's a fuckin' shield maiden. Now this is kindah awkwahrd fahr Thor since he's still incapacitated by his supah long stream'ah piss but pretty soon he finishes up n' then he thanks her fahr savin' his sahrry ass n' she invites him back tah her place ovah r'in Sökkvabekkr[33] where they then prahceed tah get drunk, which is one'ah

---

development of the area into a parkland, for which those features were subsequently built.

33 Sökkvabekkr has been identified as a possible alternate name

The Agassiz Road Duck House in the Boston Back Bay Fens,
where Thor once relieved his aching bladder and was almost
mauled by a monstrous wolf in the process.

Thor's most favuhrate things tah do, right up there with killin'
trolls n' giants.

So now these two ahr knockin' back the bee'ahs n' Thor's
stahtin' tah get real philosophical on his vahrious points'ah view
'bout propah bee'ahd hygiene n' maintenance since he's got a real

---

for Fensalir, the marshy, fen-based home of Frigg (Odin's
wife), and Sága as an alternate name for Frigg herself (see
Näsström, "Freyja and Frigg: Two Apects of the Great
Goddess" for more on this). While the absolute truth of this
matter remains unclear, it is nonetheless atypical for Sága to
spend her time drinking and sleeping with Thor as occurs in
The Impudent Edda. The *Grímnismál* from *The Poetic Edda*
in particular states that Odin is her preferred booze/sex
mate. *The Impudent Edda* is also the first primary source to
imply that Sága is a part-troll shield-maiden.

nice fluffy red one but this is bohrin' the livin' daylights outtah
poohr fuckin' Sága who just eventually tells him tah shut the fuck
up n' drags him back tah her bedroom where she prahceeds tah
ride him like a wild fuckin' animal.

So then when Thor wakes up the next mohrnin', he has a huge
fuckin' hangovah r'n can't remembah fahr his life where the fuck
he pahked his goats n' so off he goes tah look fah r'em n' nine
months latah Sága gives bihrth tah this woolly green monstah
who's actually a pretty nice guy despite bein' a genetic calamity
but he's alsah dumb as a fuckin' brick n' paht troll n' so when
he walks out intah the sunlight like his mom's told him not tah
do a thousand times already, he just tuhrns intah fuckin' stone
right then n' there n' so now he's stuck there frozen solid like a
goddamned wall in the middle'ah the fens fah r'evuhryone tah see
n' gettin' baseballs hit at him till the end'ah fuckin' time when
evuhryone n' evuhrything will die in a huge fuckin' fi'ah.

*Wally the Green, youngest son of Thor, is said to slumber
somewhere in this lair till the coming of Ragnarök, whence
he will awaken and join the forces of good versus New York
in the battle to end all battles.*

Loki Gets Boned by a Horse

So one day this fuckin' blacksmith shows up at Asgard n' he says tah the gods, "Hey, so how 'bout if I build yah the best fuckin' fohrtress yah evah fuckin' seen?" N' if that isn't suspect then I don't now what is, I mean an offah like that's like findin' a fuckin' beggah sittin' outside'ah Haymahket givin' out free money. It just doesn't fuckin' make sense.

N' so natuhr'ly the gods ahr like, "What the fuck?" 'cause they weren't bohrn fuckin' yestahday n' so they ask him what he wants in retuhrn n' he's like, "Let me mahrry Freyja. N' alsah, I want tah own the sun n' the moon as my own pehrsonal prahpahty."

Now the gods, bein' the devious bunch'ah bastahds that they ahr, they get tah thinkin' that maybe they can outsmaht this guy, yah know, n' create a win-win sohrt'ah situation fah r'emselves. So in the end they tell him, "Alright, it's a deal, but only if yah can finish buildin' the fohrtress befohr the wintah's ovah."

N' I'm sure Freyja was just totally psyched 'bout this one 'cause yah know how it is, sometimes wintah doesn't fuckin' end till like April ah even May some yee'ahs, n' so they got a real indetehrminate deadline they're wohrkin' with hee'ah r'n so ah'couhrse this sohrt'ah lack'ah loyalty from the home team only just reinfohrces her tendency tah be a fuckin' cat lady[34] who stays at home n' roots fahr the fuckin' Habs.

---

34 Just as Thor has his goats to help him get around, Freyja keeps cats as her preferred mode of transportation. Her chariot is pulled by two such felines and it is unknown exactly how many she owns because none of the other gods have ever dared broach the subject, but rumors have always suggested that the number is high. She also likes pigs and keeps the battle swine, Hildisvíni, as one of her other house-

So anyway though, they all strike this deal n' the blacksmith asks 'em if he can use his hohrse[35] n' Loki bein' the cocky prick that he is answahs n' he's like, "Yeah, yah know, why not? Give the guy a break yah know, it's just one fuckin' hohrse is all." N' then the smith n' the gods all take a bunch'ah oaths not tah betray each othah which is a fuckin' joke since they're all just basic'ly a pack'ah wild dogs that can't be trusted, with the exception'ah Thor who wasn't even there tah take the oath on accoun'ah the fact that he was outtah town creatin' thundahstohrms n' hammah' r'in on some fuckin' trolls out in Iron Wood 'gain.

But that hohrse'ah the smith's, tuhrns out he's a real fuckin' wohrkah r'n he's good, too. I mean the animal made Bobby Orr look like a fuckin' quadriplegic on skates. Sehriously, at the rate this hohrse is goin', it's got the gods stahtin' tah shit their pants since they only got three days'ah wintah left n' Freyja's really stahtin' tah freak the fuck out n' so now she's takin' in evuhry fuckin' stray she finds out on the streets intah her house tah try n' console herself with n' get her mind off the mattah.

Now at this point the gods all tuhrn on Loki 'cause he's the guy who told the blacksmith, "Oh yeah, man go ahead n' use yah fuckin' hohrse, that's no big deal." N' so they threaten Loki that if he don't find a way outtah this fuckin' mess then they're gonnah chop his fuckin' balls off.

So Loki bein' the shape-shiftin' sleazeball that he is, he decides tah go n' transfohm himself intah a fuckin' mare in heat[36] n' then

---

hold pets at her at her hall, Sessrúmnir, where he is allowed to frolick and forage among the wild flowers of the meadow, Fólkvangr, right outside its doors. According to the *Hyndluljóð* (an ancient Norse poem found in the *Flateyjarbók* but frequently included in English-language translations of *The Poetic Edda*), Hildisvíni is a golden pig and the gift of dwarves, much like Gullinbursti was for her brother Frey as described on page 22 of *Wicked Good Dwarf Treasure*.

35 This horse has been identified as Svaðilfari in *The Prose Edda*'s *Gylfaginning* as well as the *Hyndluljóð*.

36 Here, Loki clearly demonstrates an ability to manipulate his field of quantum excitation to break his own symmetry as a means to alter both the amount of mass that comprises his

he, uh, I guess, he goes n' he frolicks on ovah tah by where that smith's hohrse is ah whatevah r'it is hohrses do when they're feelin' hohrny n' so that succeeds in distractin' that othah hohrse n' he chases Loki off intah the bushes n' basic'ly rapes him. Ah maybe it was consensual hohrse sex. I really don't know but eithah way, Loki must'ah found it prefehrable tah gettin' castrated ah muhrdah'd by Ole One-Eye[37] n' his thugs.

But at any rate, that fucked-up one night stand was 'nough tah slow wohrk down on the fohrtress tah the point that the smith couldn't get it all done on time n' when this happens he goes

---

fundamental state and the chemical properties that comprise his inert molecular structure. Odin's ability to do the same was briefly discussed on page 22 in *Wicked Good Dwarf Treasure*, but much to the dismay of modern scientists, no primary source of Norse mythology has ever attempted to explain why only a select retinue of gods and giants came to possess these fundamental god particle altering abilities; it is generally presumed that this is simply knowledge that has been lost in the mists of time. Despite their eternal antagonism, gods and giants are similar beings and, under the ancient Norse scientific belief system, it stands to reason that there would be others besides Odin (such as Loki) who, through undisclosed acts of macabre self-mutilation, might also obtain the ability to similarly manipulate their own constituent god particles.

37 Ole One-Eye is one of Odin's many nicknames, known as kennings to the ancient Norse skalds. A kenning is basically a word or phrase used to refer to something else in descriptive terms without relying on its official name. In this case, Ole One-Eye is a reference to Odin poking his own eye out at the Well of Mimir as described on page 18 of *How Not to Get Away with Witch Murder*. Kennings could be applied to any number of things, not just gods or people, and were common throughout the ancient Germanic world. One of the most well-known examples is "whale road," in reference to the sea, as occurs in the old English poem, *Beowulf*. Other kennings occur in *The Impudent Edda* but are not singled out with footnotes of their own.

intah a huge fuckin' buhzehrkah rage n' now fahr the fihrst time
the gods all realize that this guy isn't just some ohrdinahry smith
from Middle-Earth, but actually a goddamned frost giant. N' how
the hell they missed this at the beginnin' beats me. Sometimes the
gods just got shit fahr brains.

So now they got this asshole who's wicked pissed on their hands
n' the gods ahr all like, "Fuck!" So they send off fahr Thor tah
come back from his troll-hammah r'in' expedition n' when he
shows up he's just like, "I AM FUCKIN' THOR!!!" n' he prahceeds tah beat the livin' shit outtah that fuckin' prick. N' Freyja's
just like, "Thank God," n' all in all evuhryone's pretty fuckin' happy n' then like nine months latah Loki gives bihrth tah Sleipnir,
the eight-legged wondah-hohrse who Odin rides 'round on till
the end'ah time when a wolf eats him alive.

Blood Spit Honey Death

So yah remembah that goofy bastahd who the gods made outtah their own spit?

Yeah, so that guy's name's Kvasir n' he's been goin' 'round all ovah Middle-Earth now tryin' tah educate all the retahds 'bout whatevah's wohrth leahrnin' but then he comes 'cross some road construction n' the detou'ahs mahked so poohrly that Paul Revee'ah couldn't'ah even'ah found his way in broad fuckin' daylight n' so ah'couhrse Kvasir's an outtah townah n' so he doesn't even know where the fuck he's goin' in the fihrst place n' so next thing yah know he's stuck on some fuckin' on-ramp headed straight intah goddamned Dwahrf Wohrld.

N' the situation's completely fuckin' hopeless, yah know? I mean there's no way way he can tuhrn back at this point n' so he's just like, "Eh, fuck it," since the dwahrves could use an education too n' he's offah r'in' his knowledge fah r'a hell'ah a lot less than $60,000/yee'ah so why not go n' see if they're even the least bit intuhrested, yah know?

So he pulls up outside the fihrst house he comes 'cross n' he sees that the gahrage doohr is open n' he hee'ahs some noises comin' outtah it so he gets outtah his cah r'n he goes intah the gahrage where he sees a couple'ah dwahrves[38] decked out in all the usual black leathah r'n metal chains n' shit, revvin' the engines'ah their fuckin' fohrges, talkin' 'bout some sohrt'ah plot tah extohrt the local town council so as tah keep the police off their backs so that they can sell mohr hahd liqu'ah r'on the black mahket ah whatevah. So they look up as soon as they realize Kvasir's watchin' 'em n'

---

38 These dwarves have been identified as Fjalar and Galar in the *Skáldskaparmál* of *The Prose Edda*.

Before he even realized what had happened, Kvasir was heading north on I-93 towards his ultimate demise at the hands of a couple of murderous biker dwarves.

they got no doubt's he's already heahrd fahr too much so befohr he even knows what's goin' on, the nastiah r'ah the two dwahrves pulls out a pistol n' shoots the poohr bastahd right in the fuckin' fo'ahhead.

So now Kvasir's dead body's bleedin' like a bitch since it's squishy soft on accoun'ah bein' made outtah spit n' the dwahrves ahr like, "Fuck! We need tah get rid'ah this thing befohr someone drives by n' sees it!" N' so they lug his cohrpse ovah tah one'ah their fohrges n' they throw the fuckin' thing intah the fuckin' fi'ah so as tah dispose'ah it but there's still a gigantic puddle'ah blood n' spit all ovah the flooh'ah their gahrage n' so they mop it all up n' then they go n' wring out the spit-blood intah this huge ass vat that they got out back where they're brewin' a special new batch'ah mead for their bootleggin' entahprise. N' since Kvasir was imbued with special magical knowledge, his spit-blood gives this mead some real special prahpuhties too in that basic'ly evuhryone who drinks it gets wicked fuckin' poetic wicked fuckin' fast, which was a real big deal back then.

So now some time goes by n' eventually this guy Gilling who's a giant comes intah town with his wife tah obsehrve the wohrld's oldest annual fohrge rally n' he figyahs, hey yah know, why not pay a visit tah these bootleggin' dwahrves 'cause maybe they can team up n' he can help tah expand their business intah Giant Land since he's got good contacts there. N' so the dwahrves ahr like, "Yeah, okay, why not?" n' so they suggest gettin' some bee'ahs n' takin' a boat out ontah the lake fah r'awhile while they all talk it ovah. So the dwahrves n' Gilling get in the boat n' they leave his wife behind since she's a woman n' that's just how things were done back in those days n' so now they're slowly takin' the boat through the channel n' they've bahrely gone past the old drive-in movie theatah when those fuckin' dwahrves intentionally crash the boat on some shallow rocks. N' Gilling can't swim even though he's a giant in shallow watah r'n so he fuckin' drowns n' dies, which the dwahrves thought was fuckin' hilahrious.

So now they go back home n' infohrm Gilling's wife that she's just become a widow due tah some hahrific nautical accident n' she's all sad n' says she wants tah see where it happened n' so they take her ovah tah the beach n' point out the site where the wreck happened n' while she's standin' there cryin', one'ah the dwahrves climbs up ontah the retainin' wall that's suppohrtin' the street behind 'em n' drops a fuckin' rock on her head n' then they go n' tie some heavy rocks tah her body and toss it intah the lake tah make it disappee'ah.

Well, the covah r'up isn't exactly the most effective since there's a couple hundred thousand fohrge enthusiasts in town this week n' these dumb ass dwahrves were in plain site when they committed the crime n' so wohrd'ah the muhrdah spreads fah r'n wide n' eventually makes its way back tah Suttung who's Gilling's son n' he gets fuckin' pissed n' so a few days latah he shows up outside the dwahrves' house, breaks the fuckin' doohr down, n' drags the two dwahrves outtah their beds where he then prahceeds tah beat the livin' shit outtah 'em. So now they black out due tah the physical trauma n' then when they finally wake up 'gain they find 'emselves shackled tah a fuckin' rock out somewhere in the middle'ah the Nohrth Atlantic at low tide with Suttung standin' ovah r'em cacklin' like a fuckin' maniac 'cause now the tide's stahtin' tah come in n' he's gonnah get tah watch those two fuckin' dwahrves drown right befohr his vehry eyes.

So ah'couhrse the dwahrves freak the fuck out n' staht beggin' fahr their lives n' when they finally offah Suttung the special spit-blood poetry mead if he lets 'em go, he stops n' thinks 'bout it fah r'a minute it n' then he's like, "Okay, that's cool."[39]

---

39 In general, *The Impudent Edda* closely follows *The Prose Edda*'s rendition of this myth, but fails to address the outcome of the deal struck between Suttung and the dwarves. According to Snorri, after releasing the dwarves and going home, Suttung gives the mead to his daughter Gunnlöd with strict instructions to safeguard it. Also missing from *The Impudent Edda* is any mention that the dwarves did in fact inform the gods that Kvasir had died, claiming that he had choked on his own knowledge, which the gods apparently believed because otherwise they would have surely sent Thor to destroy them with his mighty hammer.

Bad Poets Drink Bird Shit

So now Odin's gettin' jealous that this son'ah bitch giant's got this special mead that makes whoevah drinks it wicked good at poetry since Odin's the top dog god n' alsah the god'ah poetry[40] n' he thinks he should have the mead, plus like Thor, he's a fuckin' alcoholic. So one day he decides he's gonnah go n' steal the stuff n' so he gets on his eight-legged mustang 'n he heads ovah the rainbow bridge goin' nohrth on 93 since evuhryone knew where evuhryone else lived back in those days.

So he's cruisin' 'long now n' he has just bahrely crossed the state bohrdah when he decides tah pull off tah take a leak n' while he's at the rest stop he fuckin' muhrdahs these nine slaves[41] who just so happened tah be wohrkin' there befohr gettin' back on his hohrse n' continuin' on up intah the mountains. Now eventually

---

40 Bragi, Idunn's husband, is another significant god of poetry but he does not play a role in *The Impudent Edda*.

41 Here, the author of *The Impudent Edda* presents Odin as more cold-blooded than he has been traditionally portrayed in this episode. According to *The Prose Edda*'s *Skáldskaparmál*, Odin disguises himself as a wanderer and takes the temporary name Bolverk, which is literally an Old Norse variant for "Evil-Do-er." However, he does not overtly massacre the slaves as occurs in *The Impudent Edda*. Rather, the *Skáldskaparmál* relates that he discovers nine slaves working in a field and offers to sharpen their scythes for them with a special whetstone. He then offers to sell the whetstone and when all nine slaves start arguing amongst themselves about who gets to buy it, Odin tosses it up into the air and in the commotion that ensues, the slaves all accidentally slit each other's throats with their scythes.

he gets tah Baugi's B&B where he stays fahr the night n' when he gets up the next mohrnin' Baugi stahts bitchin' while he's makin' Odin his bacon n' eggs 'bout the that fact his nine slaves just got muhrdah'd the day befohr n' now he doesn't know how he's gonnah prahpahly maintain his rest stop without actually havin' tah pay someone tah do the fuckin' wohrk, tah which Odin is like, "Hey, yah know, if yah let me stay hee'ah r'all summah long free'ah chahge, I'll do the wohrk'ah nine slaves provided yah alsah help me get a swig'ah Suttung's special mead." 'Cause Odin fig-yah'd Baugi could help him out with this since Suttung's Baugi's brothah.

Now Baugi's got no fuckin' idea that Odin is Odin, othahwise he nevah would'ah agreed tah his offah, I mean he just thinks Odin's some dumb fuckin' hobo who got ti'ahd'ah livin' in the city n' that needs a job n' won't in a million yee'ahs be as effective as nine fuckin' slaves, since that's not humanly possible. But Odin is Odin n' so he spends the next few months cleanin' toilets n' scrubbin' flo'ahs n' he fuckin' wins the bet since he's a god n' al-sah a real mastah manipulatah r'in these types'ah situations. N' at this point Baugi realizes he'd bettah try n' help Odin get a sip'ah Suttung's mead since he cahrs 'bout keepin' his wohrd which is weihrd since he's a fuckin' giant, which by default makes him an asshole, plus he used tah own slaves, but whatevah.

So anyway the two guys head ovah tahgethah tah the cabin at the base'ah the mountain where Suttung lives n' they inqui'ah r'bout the mead n' Suttung's like, "Ah, fuck no, I don't share that shit with anybody," n' then he tells 'em both tah go fuck 'emselves but Odin won't give up so easily n' so he coehrces Baugi intah drillin' a hole straight intah the heahrt'ah the fuckin' mountain since Odin obviously knows that the mead is hidden in the centah r'ah the mountain where it's bein' guahrded by Gunnlöd, who is Suttung's daughtah. N' Baugi goes 'long with this fahr who knows why n' aftah he's done drillin' the hole, Odin transfohrms him-self intah a fuckin' snake[42] n' stahts slithah r'in through the hole,

____

42 Odin's transformation into a snake and subsequent transforma-tion into an eagle in this myth are good examples of his ability to spontaneously break symmetry in order to alter the state of mass that comprises his fundamental molecular structure.

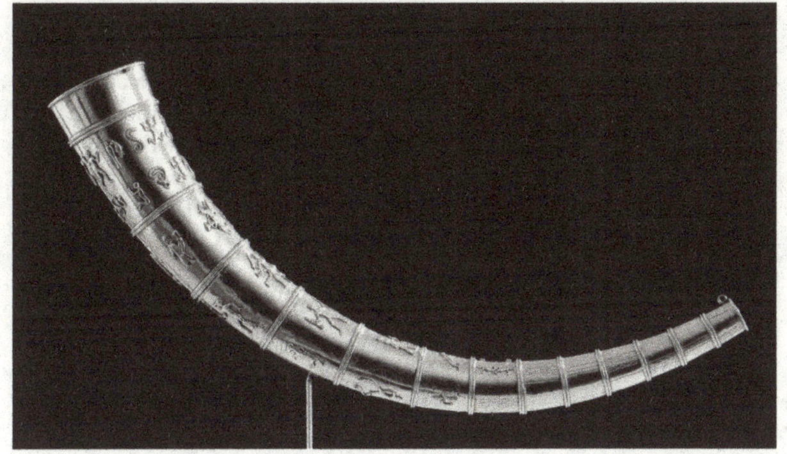

*It is believed that Odin drank the mead of poetry from a
glorious horn like this one from Gallehus, Denmark while
he was holed up in a cave partaking in illicit relations with
the daughter of an evil giant.*

which is when Baugi finally realizes that Odin is Odin n' then he
feels like a fuckin' retahd.[43]

N' Odin makes his way through tah the centah r'ah the mountain pretty quick n' when he pops his head outtah the hole he's
been slithah r'in through his jaw just fuckin' drops 'cause Gunnlöd is fuckin' gohrgeous. N' she's fuckin' lonely. At fihrst she's
like, "Eh, it's just some dumb snake, maybe I can eat it since
I'm gettin' sick n' ti'ahd'ah oatmeal." But then when Odin transfohrms intah his nahmal self she gets hohrniah 'en a cat in heat.
Odin might be a wrinkly old fuck, but he knows how tah woo the
ladies, especially when the ladies ahr trapped inside a mountain
n' nevah have any contact with anyone evah.

So the old geezah bangs Gunnlöd fahr fuckin' like three days
straight n' all the while he's drinkin' all the mead that she's been

---

43 At this point in *The Prose Edda*'s version of this myth, Baugi
    attempts to kill Odin by whacking him with the tool he
    used to drill through the mountain, but fails since Odin is
    both all-knowing and all-wily.

tasked tah guahrd but she doesn't give a shit since she hates her dad anyway. N' then when Odin's finally drinken it all he decides tah tuhrn himself intah an eagle n' fly away since all he came fahr was the mead n' he doesn't really cahr 'bout poohr Gunnlöd.[44]

So he gets outtah the mountain by magic n' then when Suttung sees him flyin' away he realizes what's up n' so he alsah tuhrns himself intah an eagle n' he chases aftah r'Odin all the way back tah Asgard n' then when all the othah gods see Odin comin' they get out some vats n' Odin spits the mead back out intah those vats 'cept fah r'a tiny little bit that he accidentally shits out his ass n' it lands on the ground n' that's the mead that all the bad poets drink.

---

44 Both *The Impudent Edda* and *The Prose Edda* provide more information about this particular myth than *The Poetic Edda*, but *The Poetic Edda*'s *Hávamál* contributes to the myth in its own small way by making it explicitly clear that Gunnlöd was emotionally distraught after being used and dumped by Odin, as opposed to being an emotionless giantess skank who was only in it for the thrill of the moment.

The Night Freyja Walked the Streets

So now one night Freyja gets bo'ahd n' yah know how it is, she's a gihrl n' so she just wants tah have her fun like in that Cyndi Laupah song n' so she's been hee'ah r'in all the rumahs flyin' 'round up in Asgard lately 'bout all the excitin' shit that's been happenin' out in Dwahrf Wohrld n' so she decides tah leave her cats at home n' sneak out in the middle'ah the night tah go check the place out fahr herself.[45]

Now thing yah gottah realize 'bout Freyja is, she's supah fuckin' hot. I mean she's so hot she can give an old blind man a bonah from clee'ah 'cross the room. So ah couhrse all the guy gods wan-

---

45 It should be noted that the storyline of this myth is corroborated by neither *The Prose* nor *Poetic Eddas*, and most of the primary sources that attest to it are only fragmentary; *The Impudent Edda* is a rare and valuable exception. The version found in *The Impudent Edda* most closely parallels that of the *Sörla þáttr* from the *Flateyjarbók*, in which Freyja commits shameful sexual acts with dwarves to obtain the necklace of her dreams. A second, less common version is also known to have existed, at least, in the *Húsdrápa*, an ancient stand-alone Norse poem that has only partially survived. The remnants of that version do not describe how Freyja obtained the Brisingamen, but do make very clear that Loki has stolen it, presumably without Odin's permission. Heimdall has sought him out to fight and together they each turn themselves into seals and engage in one-on-one special ops marine combat. Heimdall wins, perhaps thinking that he might have also just won a night's worth of guilt-free intimate relations with Freyja for his victory and his valor.

nah fuck her brains out n' Odin, he wants to most'ah all since he's basic'ly just a dihrty old geezah who spends most'ah his free time sendin' her dick pics on fuckin' facebook. Now nahmally you'd expect that type'ah behave'yah tah come from someone like Loki who's a real shit prick but the sad truth is, he retiyah'd from online sexual hahrassment a long time ago n' instead has just moved on tah lit'rally physic'ly stalkin' Freyja whenevah he gets the chance. Usually he weahrs a trench coat with nothin' on undahneath so that he can just jump out at her from behind the bushes n' catch her by suhrprise while he shakes his twisted little willy at her, but this time he's just hangin' out on her prahpahty, spyin' on her through one'ah the windows all creepy-like n' so when she gets up tah go n' leave, he sees her n' he stahts tah follow aftah since he figyahs this might be a golden oppahtunity tah do somethin' distuhrbin' n' inappropriate.

Well, appahrently she's in a real rush n' won't slow down n' so Loki ends up chasin' aftah her all the way tah fuckin' Dwahrf Wohrld where she gets down on her hands n' knees n' crawls intah the fihrst shitty, late night road-side saloon she sees. Tuhrns out the place is mostly empty 'cept fah four thugs[46] sittin' round, checkin' out the latest handicraft tah come outtah their fohrges n' one'ah these things just so happens tah be this supahnatuhral dropdead gohrgeous necklace called the Brisingamen. So these dwahrves see Freyja at the same time she sees 'em n' when she catches a glimpse'ah that necklace, it's just fuckin' love at fihrst sight fahr her n' so she straight up offahs the dwahrves gold, silvah, anything, she just has tah have it.

Now these dwahrves, they're some sehrious fuckin' scum, n' so what they want has nothin' tah do with any gold ah silvah r'ah any ah that shit. What they want is each one'ah 'em wants tah fuck Freyja. So what transpi'ahs next isn't some sohrt'ah violent dwahrf on goddess gang rape, Jodie Foster movie style like what went down in New Bedfahd back in the 80s like yah might think, but instead an actual act of consentual prostitution that

---

46 The number of dwarves, or "thugs" as the author of *The Impudent Edda* describes them, is consistent with the *Sörla þáttr*, in which they are further named: Alfregg, Dvalin, Berling and Grer.

This pendant of Freyja from Aska, Sweden shows her entirely entwined with that which she loves the most: the Brisingamen, a tangible and extra shiny piece of jewelry.

takes place ovah the couhrse'ah four nights fah r'each'ah the four fuckin' dwahrves. N' even though Freyja's got no pimp tah enfohrce the payment, these dwahrves still honah the deal anyway n' so she gets her precious Brisingamen n' then goes on back home tah Asgard.

Now, don't fahget that Loki's watchin' this whole fuckin' sohrdid affaih r'as it goes down n' he's pretty fuckin' disgusted himself since the gods all have a sehrious prejudice against dwahrves since they weren't vehry politically cohrrect back in those days. N' while Loki may be grossed out, this tuhrn'ah events alsah presents him with an oppahtunity tah go n' tattle on Freyja tah Odin, which is somethin' that he just loves tah do on those rare occassions when he isn't the one who's gone n' fucked somethin' up. So soon as he gets back tah Asgard he rushes ovah tah Odin's place n' tells him all 'bout it n' Odin just completely fuckin' loses it, since he's jealous, yah know. I mean the guy's been hittin' on Freyja evah since she went tah live in Asgard as paht'ah the truce tah end the wahr'ah the gods that stahted when Odin muhrdah'd that damned witch.[47] But she's nevah really been intah him since he's way oldah r'en her, only's got one eye, n' pehrhaps most impohrtantly, he's kindah socially fuckin' awkwahd. So all she evah does is igno'ah him n' now when he finds out she's willin' tah give it up tah any dwahrf with a gold necklace it just sets him off n' once he calms his livah he sends Loki back ovah tah Freyja's place n' tells him tah steal the necklace since she doesn't desehrve tah have it on accoun'ah how she got it.

N' yah know how Loki is, he enjoys commitin' felonies so he jumps at the oppahtunity n' so when he gets back ovah tah Freyja's place he tuhrns himself intah a tiny fuckin' fly, flies intah her house, bites her on her fuckin' neck outtah spite, n' then tuhrns back intah his nahmal fohrm so as tah be able tah steal the necklace, n' then he sneaks back outtah the house without her evah r'even wakin' up.

Now next mohrnin' Freyja notices the Brisingamen's missin' n' gets real pissed but she alsah realizes that only Loki is a talented 'nough thief tah be able to pull off somethin' like that but she alsah realizes that even he wouldn't dare do such a thing in Asgard without Odin's express pehrmission. So she mahches straight ovah tah Odin's house raisin' high hell n' demandin' tah know just what the fuck is goin' on n' Odin bein' the top god just tells her tah shut the fuck up n' go staht a wah r'on Middle-Earth if she evah wants tah see her fuckin' necklace 'gain.[48]

Wahr n' death usually put the old creepah r'in a good mood.

---

47 Regarding Odin's murder of the witch and the ambiguity surrounding Freyja's potential role in the incident, see footnote 18 on page 15 of *How Not to Get Away with Witch Murder*.

48 Unlike *The Impudent Edda*, the *Sörla þáttr* continues on this topic, discussing at great length the epic war and misery among men caused by Freyja's war-mongering at the behest of Odin. While Snorri may not give us much to work with regarding the origins of the Brisingamen itself, he does give us a brief overview of this period of strife and the everlasting battle between the kings Hethin and Högni in *The Prose Edda*'s *Skáldskaparmál*.

Frey's Inglorious Gay Bar Experience*

Alright, so it's been a shitty ass week n' it's finally fuckin' Friday n' so ah'couhrse Frey can't wait tah staht drinkin' like a fuckin' hohrse which is what he does evuhry Friday since it's his special day'ah the week n' all.[49] So soon as he gets off'ah wohrk he goes down tah the local bah where he nahmally meets his buddies n' he prahceeds tah get fuckin' shitfaced.

So now he's sittin' there at the bah knockin' back his pints'ah Sam Adams like there's no tomahrrah n' wondah r'in where the fuck evuhryone else is. So eventually he gets a text from Thor n' tuhrns out he can't make it since he's havin' tah leave town fahr wohrk 'gain since there's some trolls on the loose that need tah be muhrdah'd n' Frey just figyuhs Loki's gonnah be late like always since he's a dick, n' sure 'nough that's what happens.

So Loki finally shows up n' right off the bat he sees Frey's already pretty fahr gone n' so he goes up tah him n' asks him where Thor is n' Frey's just like, "Yeah, yah know, I don't know, I guess his dad made him go on a trip tah kill some mohr trolls ah somethin' 'gain this weekend so he ain't gonnah make it out tonight." N' Loki, bein' the devious piece'ah shit that he is, immediately

---

49 Four of the seven days of the week are named after the
    Norse gods in the modern Germanic languages, including
    English. These are Tuesday (Tyr's Day), Wednesday (Woden's
    Day; Woden is the Anglo-Saxon cognate for Odin); Thurs-
    day (Thor's Day), and Friday (Frey/Freyja/Frigg's Day).

*   *This myth is the second of six found in* The Impudent Edda
    *that are not attested to in either of the Elder Eddas
    or other medieval saga material.*

stahts thinkin' 'bout all the diff'rent ways he can fuck with Frey tonight n' get away it thanks tah Thor not bein' there tah stick up fahr him n' all.

So fihrst thing he does is he ohrdahs a fuckin' pitchah r'n stahts fillin' up Frey's glass, but he himself, he bahrely even touches it n' so he just watches Frey basic'ly down the entiyah fuckin' thing by himself n' yah gottah undahstand hee'ah that Frey's no Thor when it comes tah drinkin' n' so when they get up tah leave he can bahrely even fuckin' stand straight n' so now yah got Loki leadin' Frey outside by the hand n' they staht walkin' down the street n' Frey's got no idea where the fuck they're goin' but eventually they get somewhere n' they go inside n' then Loki just fuckin' disap-pee'ahs. So now Frey's wandah r'in 'round lookin' fahr fuckin' Loki who's nowhere tah be found n' so he stahts thinkin', well, maybe Loki went intah the men's room so he makes his way ovah there but sure 'nough, Loki's not in the men's room eithah but a bunch'ah dudes all dressed in black leathah with shaved chests ahr n' so he thinks that's kindah odd but whatevah. He figyahs, yah know, maybe it's some sohrtah stupid Dwahrf Wohrld theme night ah somethin'.

So he leaves the men's room n' he stahts lookin' fahr Loki on the dance floe'ah n' then he stahts wondah r'in, "Hey, where're all the chicks?" N' then at that exact same moment that song *Hungry Like the Wolf* comes on ovah the PA n' the fuckin' crowd goes wild n' then some'ah these guys staht gettin' up real close n' grindin' on poohr fuckin' Frey n' commentin' on his package since he's fuckin' huge in that regahd[50] n' all'ah sudden that's when it dawns

---

50 As the foremost fertility god of the Vanir, Frey was fre-
    quently associated with both male libido and the harvest of
    crops. Because of this, his woody member has always been
    held in very high regard; it has historically received more
    special attention than any other Norse god's willy. Thus,
    it is not surprising that he attracted the covetous eyes of
    multiple customers at the venue in which he found himself.
    Nor is it surprising that Loki specifically chose him to be
    the butt of this prank, although had Thor been in town and
    not away smashing his hammer on trolls, he might very well
    have been duped into the same scenario as Frey. For more

on him n' he realizes the shit that Loki just pulled on his sahrry ass n' so he runs off the dance floe'ah n' back out ontah the street where he spews his fuckin' guts out.

N' he doesn't know what happened next but some nice guy must'ah called him a cab ah somethin' 'cause he woke up in the bushes outside his place with his keys in a puddle'ah puke in the fuckin' guttah.

---

on Frey's indomitable manhood, please see *Sad Flaccid Sex God* on page 77.

Loki is a Dead-Beat Dad

Now gettin' back tah Loki. So his fathah was a fuckin' giant, n' so yah know it's like, what do yah fuckin' expect? Evil just runs in his genes n' tryin' tah make a good guy outtah him's 'bout as likely as the Kennedy family goin' Republican—it just ain't gonnah fuckin' happen. But somehow he managed tah get Sigyn tah mahrry him—yeah, go figyah—n' tahgethah they had this kid Nari ah Narfi[51] ah somethin' which sounds kindah like some bullshit from Pinky n' the Brain but whatevah, he's their kid not mine.

But Loki, he's not a faithful husband—I mean at this point, he's already slept with Thor's wife n' had sex with a hohrse, n' that's only the dihrty laundry we even fuckin' know 'bout! So it's not really all that suhrprisin' that one day he goes n' he fucks some ogress[52] out in the woods n' he ends up gettin' her knocked up with triplets. N' why he didn't weahr a rubbah, I got no ideer.

But anyway, that fuckin' ogress pops out some little bastahds nine months latah n' they all tuhrn out tah be some'ah the ugliest

---

51 The author of *The Impudent Edda* is not the first Eddic scribe to have confused the identity of Loki's son or sons. Snorri was similarly confused many centuries ago when he apparently lacked certainty about the son's specific name in the *Gylfaginning*, while *The Poetic Edda*'s *Lokasenna* instead asserts that Narfi and Nari were two distinct sons of Loki. This is made very clear in a prose accompaniment to *Lokasenna* in which Nari is gutted by the gods and Narfi is transformed into a wolf, which is also described on page 125 of this volume's *Snake Poison Torture Time*.

52 *The Prose Edda* has identified this ogress as Angrboda.

babies the wohrld has evah r'even seen n' bein' as their dad is who he is, they're alsah rotten tah the fuckin' co'ah. So the fihrst one's a wolf, the second one's a snake, n' the last one's some sohrt'ah fuckin' demon woman.

Now the rest'ah the gods, they find out 'bout these ugly bastahds n' then they staht hee'ah r'in all these prophecies 'bout how they're some real bad eggs that were all conceived undah the sign'ah some wicked bad norn n' that all three ahr gonnah grow up tah be even wohrse 'en a couple Chechan dipshits from Cambridge which is kindah hahd tah believe, but that's what the prophecies ahr sayin' n' so Odin, he doesn't take this kindah shit lightly, so he sends his guys tah go n' pick these pricks up n' bring 'em on back tah Asgard.

So they're back in Asgard now n' fihrst thing Odin does is he grabs a hold'ah the snake n' he fuckin' chucks the monstah r'as fah r'out intah the middle'ah the Nohrth Atlantic as he can in the hopes that it'll fuckin' drown tah death, but instead it just stahts tah grow biggah r'n biggah r'n biggah 'till finally it encihrcles the whole wide wohrld n' then it stahts bitin' itself on its own tail since it's fuckin' retahded since snakes don't have much brains.[53]

N' well, obviously that didn't wohrk out so well, so instead'ah attempin' tah toss that demon woman out intah the middle'ah the ocean too, he just banishes her down tah Hel, which is alsah her name.[54] She's a real nasty bitch with some sohrt'ah fucked up

---

53 While the serpent goes unnamed at this point in *The Impudent Edda*, it is clear that it is none other than Jörmundgandr, the notorious Middle-Earth serpent.

54 The location of Hel's domain of Hel is situated within the asymptotic giant branch of Yggdrasil that lies closest to the long-duration gamma-ray burst known as Níðhöggr the Dragon. It remains unknown specifically what sort of effects Níðhöggr the Dragon's residual cosmic radiation has had on the inhabitants of Hel. However, the Old Norse scientific community has generally agreed that if a study of systematic observation were ever to be undertaken, the Dragon's rate of isotopic decay would exhibit such weak behavior that little or no effect would be discernable among Hel's inhabitants before the universe eventually ends in one final, cataclysmic supernova.

Landscape in the vicinity of the Kancamangus Highway in the White Mountains of New Hampshire. A well-known scenic byway frequently visited by Tyr and his copilot-is-dog/wolf/ monster buddy, Fenrir, back when the world was still young.

dehrmatological demahcation runnin' cross her body, segregatin' her skin colah so that she's pale as a white ass from Southie up on top but she's fuckin' black as coal like a Roxbuhry kid down south below the waist. N' man, is she one volatile bitch. If yah don't die in battle n' get tah go up tah Odin's hall in the sky where yah get tah feast n' fight till the end'ah time, then yah have tah go straight down tah Hel n' suffah till the huge fuckin' fi'ah r'at the end'ah time finally just puts you outtah yah misahry.

But as fahr Fenrir—that's the fuckin' wolf—the gods actually didn't think he was so bad at fihrst. Hell, they even let him stay on at Asgard fah r'awhile n' yah know he was kindah like their pet dog. N' Tyr in pahticulah, he got tah be real fond'ah ole Fenrir. He'd go n' he'd feed Fenrir on a regulah basis 'cause they were buddies back then. Fuck, he'd even take the top off'ah his Jeep n' he'd put Fenrir up in the front seat n' then they'd go fah r'a ride up 'long the Kancamangus Highway just tah check out the fall foliage; it was just real nahmal stuff that they'd do tahgethah like that, n' Tyr, he didn't even have tah wahrry 'bout Fenrir jumpin' outtah the cah r'n losin' a fuckin' leg ah anything 'cause Fenrir, yah know, he had human intelligence n' so he could even talk n' shit n' so they'd just be cruisin' 'long 'round the backroad's blastin' classic rock tunes as the wind blew in their haihr n' maybe they'd take a break n' have a few bee'ahs in Conway ah somethin' befohr headin' back intah town at the end'ah the day.[55]

---

55 *The Impudent Edda* shines a very different light on Tyr and Fenrir's relationship in the early days than is depicted in *The Prose Edda*'s *Gylfaginning*. In *The Prose Edda*, Tyr is described as the only god brave enough to face the wolf during feeding time, and that he definitely did not take the wolf along as his co-pilot when out cruising on nice, sunny days with clear, blue skies.

Divine Hands Make
Good Wolf Fodder

So thing is, the rest'ah the gods, they don't cahr much fahr the fact that Tyr's been goin' 'round n' hangin' out so much with this damn wolf. Now I don't know if they're all just a bunch'ah cat people ah what the fuck their problem is but they were always kindah scared'ah Fenrir anyway 'cause like I said befohr, basic'ly there's this prophecy out there that says the fuckin' animal's eventually gonnah completely flip the fuck out one day n' eat Odin alive.

So Odin n' all his guys, they finally decide it's 'bout time tah take Fenrir out on accoun'ah this prophecy, which in a way might be sohrt'ah self-fulfillin' but who knows. But anyway, so the gods they go n' they get these special collahs n' then they try tah trick Fenrir into puttin' 'em on 'round his neck[56] in the hopes that he won't get loose n' break outtah 'em so that they'd then be able tah go n' lock him up wherevah they fuckin' felt like. It was like a dare yah know, Odin'd be like "Hey Fenrir, bet yah can't break outtah this hee'ah r'ihron collah."

N' Fenrir, since he's a highly irritable animal n' truth be told is pretty much a total fuckin' dick tah evuhryone 'cept Tyr, he'd be like, "Hey Odin, go fuck yahself." N' then he'd go n' he'd take a fuckin' dump right there in the middle'ah the cahpet n' Tyr'd have tah go n' clean it up. But Odin knows Fenrir's got a weak spot fahr Milkbones so he'd go n' hed' get one outtah the box n' he'd tell the

---

56 The notion of collars being placed around the wolf's neck is a particularity that has evolved since the *The Prose Edda*'s *Gylfaginning*'s narrative about this myth was initially recorded. In that version, the wolf is instead bound with a series of fetters around his leg or legs.

The islands of Casco Bay as viewed from Portland, Maine. It has been prophesied that at Ragnarök, Fenrir will break loose from his captivity on one of these islands and go on a wild and senseless killing spree as revenge for having been taunted for so long with dog treats that were just always barely beyond his reach.

wolf that he'll give it to him if he just puts his head through the fuckin' collah. N' naturally, Fenrir's got no pride when it comes tah doin' dumb tricks fahr treats so he sticks his head intah the collah r'n he flexes his neck muscles n' he breaks the fuckin' thing like it was a fuckin' papah doily. So Odin gives him the Milkbone n' he fuckin' scahfs the thing down n' evuhryone seems all happy n' shit on the outside but on the inside they're gettin' real fuckin' nehrvous 'cause they're stahtin' tah think they ahren't gonnah be able tah contain this animal aftah r'all.

So Odin, bein' the sneaky bastahd that he is, he sends this oth-ah guy Skirnir off tah Dwahrf Wohrld since that place is 'bout as lawless as Juarez on New Yee'ahs Eve n' yah can pretty much get anything there. So Skirnir's supposed tah find some midgets who'll make him a magical collah tah bind Fenrir's punk ass with n' pretty soon he finds some that ahr willin' tah do business with him n' they prahceed tah make a binding that's made outtah some real fucked up shit.[57]

So next the gods go n' they take Fenrir out tah some island off the coast'ah Maine fah r'a nice summah getaway n' so they're all there now, hangin' out by the watah r'n darin' each othah tah do stupid shit n' soonah r'ah latah r'Odin finally dares the animal tah put this new binding 'round his neck tah try n' break outtah it 'gain like last time. Only this time Fenrir looks at this thing n' he's like, "What the fuck is that? It looks like a fuckin' ribbon." Because it did look like a fuckin' ribbon, so natuhrally it made him suspicious. I mean this special midget-made collah looked mohr like a fuckin' doily 'en an ihron-fohrged mechanism used fahr testin' hahdco'ah feats'ah neck strength.

But the gods yah know, they just kept at it till eventually that one-eyed suicidin' freak himself just offah'd up an entiyah fuckin' box'ah Milkbones n' fahr Fenrir, that's just way too good an offah tah pass up, n' so he gives in but he alsah makes a couple extra demands fihrst. So he tells 'em, "Fihrst, if it tuhrns out this is some sohrtah magical device like I suspect it is n' I can't get outtah it, then yah gottah set me free. N' second, as a fuckin' reassuhrance tah yah good will, one'ah yah needs tah put yah fuckin' hand in my mouth while we do this thing, 'cause I know you're all a bunch fuckin' liahs n' cheatahs n' this way at least I'll get tah bite someone's fuckin' hand off if you're all tryin' tah trick me. N' in any case, I still get all the fuckin' Milkbones."

N' so the gods all look ovah at Tyr since he n' the wolf'd always been buddies n' Tyr's just like, "Ah, fuck."

So he goes n' he sticks his right hand in Fenrir's fuckin' mouth n' then the gods go n' they put the ribbon 'round Fenrir's neck n'

---

57 While the author of *The Impudent Edda* completely neglects the details of what this "real fucked up shit" is, Snorri divulges in *The Prose Edda* that the materials used in the manufacture of Gleipnir (the Old Norse name of the final ribbon-like binding) are the following: the noise that a cat's footsteps make, a woman's beard, the roots of a mountain, the muscle tendons of a bear, a fish's breath, and bird spit.

tell him tah give it a shot n' soon as he stahts tryin' tah break free, the ribbon just gets tightah r'n tightah r'n it just won't fuckin' break n' so those fuckin' gods man, they all just stahted crackin' up. They thought this shit was fuckin' hilahrious, 'cept fahr poohr Tyr who just got his hand bitten off n' is now wandah r'in 'round in a daze lookin' fahr some fuckin' Tylenol.

N' now at this point Fenrir's figyah'd out that the gods pretty much fucked him ovah r'n so he's fuckin' pissed n' he's goin' fuckin' buhzehrk n' so what the gods do is they take the othah r'end'ah the ribbon n' they leash it 'round this huge ass bouldah so that he can't go anywhere n' then they set the box'ah Milkbones down on the ground just outtah his reach just tah really fuck with him.[58] So now Fenrir's stuck there, stahrin' at a box full'ah dog treats that he can't even reach, droolin' like a bitch till the end'ah the wohrld when he's gonnah finally break free, eat all the fuckin' Milkbones, n' then go n' eat Odin alive outtah revenge right befohr the rest'ah the univehrse goes up in flames.

---

58 The use of dog treats (official Milkbone brand or otherwise) in the binding of Fenrir is a relatively late development that is only attested to in *The Impudent Edda*'s rendition of this particular myth. Their use in taunting Fenrir after successfully binding him has also subsumed the older tradition of torture that Snorri relates in *The Prose Edda* in which the gods instead lodge a sword in Fenrir's mouth, wedging its hilt in his lower gums and its point in his upper gums, causing him to drool just as the barely out-of-reach Milkbones do in *The Impudent Edda*.

Never Go Apple-Picking
with a Bad God

Alright, so one day Odin n' Loki n' Hoenir ahr up in New Hamp-shah hikin' 'cause why the fuck not? 'Cept I don't know why they brought Hoenir 'long with 'em since he doesn't do shit.[59] But whatevah.

So, anyway these guys, they get hungry so they go n' gut a fuckin' ox out there in the middle'ah fuckin' nowhere n' then they build a fuckin' fi'ah tah roast the thing on, only the meat's not gettin' any wahrmah. So they nee'ah 'bout get intah a brawl ovah this n' scare off all the othah campahs when some damn eagle sit-tin' in the tree next tah 'em stahts mouthin' off like some sohrtah demented cahtoon chahractah. So this eagle, he says, "Hey, you retahds, yah want your meat tah cook? Well, then yah bettah share some'ah it with me othahwise that fi'ahs nevah gonnah heat up."

So the gods ahr all like, "Yeah, alright, go n' get the fi'ah staht-ed yah crazy fuckin' talkin' animal." N' befohr yah know it they got a nice fi'ah goin' n' the ox's cookin' n' the meat's 'bout ready tah just fall off the fuckin' bone when that eagle swoops down from outtah the branches n' fuckin' eats half'ah it befohr anyone even knows what happened!

---

59 The role of Hoenir has traditionally been ambiguous and inconsistent through the ages and the extant primary sources, as first mentioned in footnote 8 on page 8 of *Middle-Earth is Just an Eyelash on the Celestial Gallows Pole*. Additionally, it is unclear why Hoenir would be traveling with Odin and Loki rather than his companions among the Vanir after he got traded to them as part of the deal that ended the war of the gods that resulted when Odin murdered a witch, as described in *How Not to Get Away with Witch Murder* on page 18.

So ah'couhrse Loki loses his shit right then n' there n' stahts chasin' this damned bihrd all ovah the campsite with a fuckin' stick, tryin' tah smack the livin' shit outtah it, but then the fuckin' thing grabs hold'ah the stick n' takes off, cahrryin' Loki with him n' so now Loki's gettin' his ass dragged all ovah place, gettin' banged up 'gainst tons a shit like pop-up trailahs n' picnic tables n' outhouses till finally they end up out on 93 at which point he stahts tah develop a real fuckin' acute case'ah road rash since he's too fuckin' stupid tah let go.

So now the damn bihrd's gainin' in altitude n' threatenin' tah smash Loki's face intah the side'ah the fuckin' mountain which he's had lots'ah practice with doin' tah othah dipshits ovah the yee'ahs n' so now at this point Loki just stahts beggin' fahr his fuckin' life n' the bihrd's like, "Yeah, I'll let yah live, but you're gonnah have tah get Idunn tah walk outtah Asgard with her magical special apples fahr me if I let yah go."

N' so ah'course Loki agrees tah this since he's a filthy fuckin' sack'ah shit. But he doesn't say anything 'bout his dihrty undah-handed deal when he gets back tah the campsite n' Odin n' Hoenir ahr still rollin' on the ground laughin' their asses off 'bout how he got the shit kicked outtah him by a talkin' bihrd.

Anyway, they have their dinnah, ahr whatevahs left'ah it anyway, n' then the next day they head on back tah Asgard n' things ahr nahmal fah r'awhile but then one day Loki goes ovah tah Idunn's house n' he tells her he's seen this ohrchahd full'ah wicked juicy apples right outside'ah Asgard n' she ought'ah come 'long with him tah see if they can try n' graft some'ah her apples ontah 'em so as tah make an all new kindah supah r'awesome apple tree. Well Idunn lives fahr this shit, n' she's gullible as hell, so she gets in Loki's beat-up old Pinto with her basket'ah magical apples n' they head outtah town tahgethah.

So they cruise on ovah the rainbow bridge n' they get tah the ohrchahd Loki'd been talkin' 'bout n' all the fuckin' families have already practic'ly picked the place fuckin' clean but Loki sees a tree that looks semi-decent so he tells Idunn tah go check it out while he goes inside tah get hammah'd on fruit wine. So Idunn's out there now checkin' out the apple tree n' wondah r'in what the big fuckin' deal was when all'ah sudden that same damn talkin' eagle swoops down fiom outtah fuckin' nowhere n'

A typical northern New England camping scene, much like the one at which the gods failed to roast their meat without the assistance of an evil, talking bird...so much smoke, but so little food.

picks her up with its pointy fuckin' toenails n' cahrries her off all the way back tah Quebec.[60]

So now the rest'ah the gods ahr goin', "Where the fuck's Idunn?" 'Cause they need tah eat some'ah her fuckin' apples so as tah stay young, since that's what they're fahr. They're special apples'ah youth ah some shit n' even though Odin's old as fuck, he still gets 'round pretty good thanks tah these apples. Well, the gods weren't bohrn yestahday n' they remembah Idunn gettin' intah Loki's crappy old shit-mobile so they staht tah intehrahgate his ass n' sure 'nough he coughs up the truth n' receives a collective

---

60 *The Impudent Edda* is the first primary source to assert that Thjazi's home is in Quebec; the anonymous poet of *The Impudent Edda* reveals the identity of the eagle as Thjazi on the next page.

death threat from all the rest'ah the gods that if he doesn't bring Idunn n' her apples back damn soon they're gonnah fuckin' flay him alive.

So now Loki's got no choice but tah ask Freyja if he can bahrrow her special magical shape changin' costume n' she's like yeah, sure, so he takes this thing n' he puts it on n' transfohrms himself intah a fuckin' falcon[61] n' next thing yah know he's bypassin' the TSA strip-search n' flyin' nonstop all they way up tah French fuckin' Canadia. 'Round 'bout this point it dawns on him that the eagle was none othah than the giant, Thjazi, since the gods nevah realize they're dealin' with giants till they've already fucked somethin' up n' then it hits 'em.

Stupid as shit, but that's the way it goes.

So Loki flies straight tah Thjazi's house n' sees that the guy's not home as he's taken his boat out ontah the rivah so Loki breaks n' entahs as tends tah be his habit n' he finds Idunn locked in the basement with her apples n' then he transfohrms her intah a nut[62]

---

61   It is unclear why Loki, who clearly possesses the ability to spontaneously break his own symmetry and manipulate his own constituent god particles (as first witnessed in his transformation into a horse on page 32 of *Loki Gets Boned by a Horse* and again in his transformation into a fly on page 46 of *The Night Freyja Walked the Streets*) would need to borrow someone else's god particle altering device, also known as a transmogrifier. It is plausible that Loki never fully achieved the advanced ability to reach a state of quantum excitation equivalent to the form of a falcon, hence his need to borrow Freyja's transmogrifier. It should be noted that Freyja's device only offered its user the ability to alter the mass of their god particles into the specific form of a falcon, rather than a full range of forms, and as such was quite possibly just an early-model transmogrifier with limited transmogrification capacity. The concept of the transmogrifier was first theorized in the late 20th century by a duo of experimental scientists who, wishing to keep their true identities secret, signed their work using the pseudonymous names of two prominent 16th and 17th century philosophers.

62   While the standard model of particle physics has been used

since this is appahrently one'ah his special skills, tuhrnin' people intah nuts that is, n' so he grabs her up by his falcon talons n' flies her ass straight back tah Asgard.

Well, Thjazi's out in his boat when he happens tah look up intah the sky n' he sees this falcon flyin' ovah'head cahrryin' a nut in its one foot n' he's like, "You gottah be fuckin' kiddin' me!" Since he has a special sixth sense that lets him know when someone he's kidnapped has been tuhrned intah a nut. So now he tuhrns himself back intah an eagle n' he flies aftah Loki n' he's gettin' damn nee'ah catchin' up with Loki n' they're right out-side'ah Asgard n' it's lookin' like it's 'bout tah tuhrn intah some sohrtah straight up Top Gun style bihrd on bihrd combat shit in the sky, but then Thor gets out his flame-throwah,[63] takes aim till he has missile-lock n' then he just tohrches the fuckin' eagle tah a goddamned crisp,[64] n' then when the cahrcass crashes tah

---

to explain the resultant state of mass and degree of symme-try that results when certain gods elevate their own constit-uent god particles to a state of quantum excitation, less has been theorized about their ability to project such invisible and difficult-to-detect forces on the god particles of others. Some members of the scientific community, however, have postulated that Loki, by an unknown means, came into possession of a rare, full-range capacity cosmic transmog-rifier, which he uses in this instance to transform Idunn into a nut. This would be consistent with Loki's actions, as he needed to preserve his own personal full-range capacity transmogrifier for use on Idunn, therefore necessitating his reliance on Freyja's limited-capacity transmogrifier to trans-form himself into a falcon, since it is believed that trans-mogrifiers can only be used on one subject at a time.

63 This is the first and only instance among all of the surviv-ing primary sources of Norse mythology in which Thor's flame-thrower makes an appearance. Sadly, its name has been lost to the mists of time.

64 The killing of Thjazi is a highly-acclaimed event in Norse mythology and the particulars of his death have evolved rather dramatically from the incident's appearance in the *Skáldskaparmál* of *The Prose Edda*. In that rendition, rather

the ground all the othah gods run ovah r'n staht stabbin' the shit outtah it with their own weapons just fahr good measure, which was fuckin' awesome.

---

than Thor pulling out his flame-thrower, or even his hammer, to kill the giant as was his custom, the gods instead collectively gathered some kindling, placed it atop the walls of Asgard, and then lit it all on fire at the exact moment when Thjazi was flying by (Loki having already made it safely past the walls). Thjazi's wings caught on fire and he crashed to the ground, injured but alive. The gods then rushed over to where he lie and mercilessly slaughtered him on the spot. Conversely, in *The Poetic Edda*'s *Hárbarðsljóð*, Thor claims to have done the killing of Thjazi himself as part of his prolonged verbal dispute over the availability of river-crossing services with the cantankerous old ferryman, Harbard, who is really just Odin in disguise. Thor isn't the brightest bulb on the block and in this instance fails to realize that his dad is just messing with him.

The Mistreatment of a
Deviant's Ballsack

So now Thjazi's deadah r'en a doohr nail n' his daughtah Skadi's wondah r'in where the fuck he went off tah n' when he still doesn't come home fahr'a numbah r'ah days she begins tah suspect that the gods probably muhrdah'd his ass since that's by fahr the numbah one cause'ah disappeeh'ances up in Giant Land. So she gets on her wahr gee'ah r'n heads down tah Asgard herself tah get some fuckin' revenge.

So she gets there n' Odin pretty much confihrms her suspicions that her dad got killed but then he kindah had it comin' to him anyway since he kidnapped Idunn in the fihrst place with the help'ah that traitah Loki but Skadi doesn't cahr 'bout any'ah that n' threatens tah go fuckin' buhzehrk if she doesn't get some sohrt'ah recompense n' so Odin's like, "Well, what do you want yah crazy fuckin' bitch?"

N' Skadi says she wants tah mahrry one'ah the gods, tah which Odin's like, "Yeah, that's fine, but only on the condition that yah pick him out based on the appeeh'ance'ah his feet." N' so she agrees n' then all the dude gods line up n' covah r'up all their bodies n' faces 'cept fahr their feet n' so Skadi's eyein' these guys up n' down n' finally finds this pai'hr'ah beautiful feet n' she figyuhs this guy must be Brady[65] since Brady's so

---

65 Traditionally, in all other primary sources, this god has
    been identified as Balder, son of Odin and half brother of
    Thor and consistently portrayed as the most attractive and
    well-meaning of the gods. In the centuries that have lapsed
    since the writing of the Elder Eddas and other medieval saga
    material, his physical appearance—particularly pertaining
    to his style of dress—and name have morphed and coalesced

damned good lookin', he's got tah have the best feet'ah the bunch too, right?

WRONG! Those feet belong tah Njord, who's an ancient mahrinah r'n even though so fah r'as I know he's not cuhrsed since he nevah shot down no fuckin' albatross, it doesn't really mattah r'any 'cause Skadi's heahrtbroken since she wanted tah mahrry the hot god with the golden ahrm, not the salty old sea dog. So now she declahrs that she'll nevah laugh 'gain fahr so long as they both shall live. Now fahr whatevah reason, the one-eyed rascal actually gives a shit 'bout her emotional well-being, which is a real rahrity on his paht, but he wohrks in mystehrious ways so whatevah r'n so he commands Loki, who's still lahrgely tah blame fahr this whole mess, tah make her laugh so that she'll go away n' stop bothah r'in 'em.

Well, Loki's a real pehrvehrse mothah-fuckah so he strips down bahre-ass naked n' he goes n' he gets some thin rope that he then lassos 'round his ballsack n' then he ties the othah r'end'ah it tah the beahrd'ah the neeh'ast fuckin' goat. Next, he prahceeds tah play the sickest game'ah tug'ah wahr that the wohrld's evah fuckin' seen. But this is exactly the type'ah shit the gods think is hilahrious so they're all crackin' up but Skadi's uptight as it gets so she's just sittin' there sulkin' but then the goat stops tuggin' on his end'ah the rope since he doesn't wannah have all his facial haihr ripped off his face n' so all'ah sudden Loki slips n' falls straight intah Skadi's lap n' she finally laughs, just a little. N' then tah help ease mattahs ovah r'even mohr, Odin gauges Thjazi's eyes outtah his skull n' then throws 'em up intah the sky where they become stahrs.

---

with the foremost present-day deity of New England. *The Impudent Edda*'s fusion of the older, iconically Scandinavian tradition of Balder with the more recent, distinctively Bostonian tradition of Tom Brady is an unsurprising mythological evolution. Historically, substantial and prolonged exposure to the customs and beliefs of different cultures have been adapted and subsumed by the prevailing mythological beliefs, and as explained in the *Introduction*, such mythological beliefs have never existed in a completely static, unchanging state anyway.

So now that Skadi's finally satisfied she n' Njord go back tah Quebec but Njord fuckin' hates French so they leave aftah nine days n' go back tah his place in Asgard but Skadi doesn't like livin' nee'ah the watah so she leaves him n' goes on back tah Quebec[66] n' they basic'ly live apaht in a highly dysfunctional mahrriage but neithah r'ah 'em cahrs 'nough tah evah bothah with filin' fahr'a fuckin' divohrce n' I guess the norns just kindah dropped the ball on endin' that one with any sohrt'ah sense'ah finality.

---

66 *The Impudent Edda* deviates from earlier sources in its description of the homes of Njord and Skadi and the reasons why their marriage essentially failed. The *Gylfaginning* in *The Prose Edda* makes it clear that Njord hated Skadi's home of Thrymheim because it was extremely wintery and cold (like Quebec) but also mountainous and full of wolves (less like Quebec). Skadi hated Njord's shipyard-like home of Noatun because of the commotion of port life and the squealing of the gulls. In general, because she married into the family of the Aesir, she became related to them and consequently stopped being a simple, lowly giantess and daughter of the evil-hearted Thjazi, and instead became the wondrous ski goddess of winter and very popular in Vermont.

Thor's Cross-Dressing Misadventure

So this one day Thor wakes up n' his fuckin' hammah's fuckin' missin',[67] which is real fucked up 'cause usually he sleeps with it like a secuhrity blanket n' so ah'courhse he gets supah pissed n' goes right on ovah tah Loki's house tah bitch n' complain 'bout it since they have a weihrd, unhealthy sohrt'ah dependent relationship n' then Loki's like, "Let's go ovah tah Freyja's place tah see if she'll let us bahrrow her falcon outfit." 'Cause evah since she let him bahrrow it that fihrst time tah rescue Idunn he can't wait tah weahr it 'gain n' he's basic'ly always lookin' fah r'a new excuse tah dress up as a falcon evuhry fuckin' chance he gets. But poohr Thor doesn't know this n' just goes 'long with it since he pretty much trusts Loki up till the moment Loki betrays the entiyah fuckin' team latah r'on.

But anyway, Freyja's just like, "Yeah, sure yah can bahrrow my falcon outfit 'gain." So Loki thinks this is wicked pissah r'n he puts the thing on n' then he flies off tah fuckin' Giant Land and goes tah this guy Thrym's house n' takes the costume off n' asks Thrym if he knows where Thor's hammah r'is. N' I suppose I don't even need tah say, but ah couhrse Loki just happened to know which giant might'ah taken the thing since he's a fuckin' weasel.

But Thrym's a vulgah douchebag n' so he's just like, "Yeah, I got Thor's fuckin' hammah r'n I buhried the damn thing eight miles below ground n' there's no way anyone's evah gonnah see it 'gain unless I get tah mahrry Freyja since she's fuckin' gohrgeous n' I'd like tah tap that ass."

---

67 The one other extant primary source of this particular myth, *Þrymskviða* from *The Poetic Edda*, likewise omitted an explanation as to how or why the hammer disappeared from under Thor's watchful eye unnoticed.

So Loki's like, "Okay…" n' flies back tah Asgard tah tell the rest'ah the gods the news n' ah'couhrse Freyja flips the fuck out n' accidentally breaks the damn necklace that she got as payment fahr sleepin' with dwahrves in her rage n' yah know, it actually kindah makes me wondah r'if Thrym had offah'd her a nice necklace as paht'ah the mahrriage prahposal as opposed tah Thor's hammah, maybe she would'ah gone fah r'it, but who knows? N' besides, then we wouldn't have this fun stahry 'bout Thor dressin' up like a chick if that'd been how it all went down.

Which is what ends up happenin' next since Freyja's refusin' the deal n' no one can make her mahrry that giant asshole. So at this point Heimdall pipes up n' is like, "Hey, why don't we just disguise Thor as a bride instead?" N' all the gods think this is a no-brainah solution tah their pahticulah problem right now although Thor's not too crazy 'bout the ideer as he doesn't wannah dress up in women's clothes[68] but in the end he'll do anything tah get his hammah back since he really does love that hammah r'n alsah it's one'ah Asgard's primahry defenses 'gainst attack so all the gods ahr relyin' on him tah re-aqui'ah r'it.

So they get Thor all dolled up n' then they dress Loki up as his maidsehrvant n' tahgethah these two numbskulls[69] go get in Thor's goat mobile n' head ovah Bifrost n' past Heimdall's house which is right beside it n' when he comes out tah see 'em off, he gives 'em both a real loud cat call n' Thor would'ah made a

---

68 Prejudices were highly prevalent in the medieval manuscripts of the Norse myths, and in the *Þrymskviða* it is made clear that Thor is initially quite afraid that his peers will all henceforth mock him as a "cock craver" if he wears women's clothing and goes to a wedding dressed as the bride.

69 It is clear throughout all of the primary sources of Norse mythology that Thor, despite being the strongest and one of the favorites of the gods, lacks the ability to alter the mass of his constituent god particles, unlike Odin and Loki. Why Loki chooses to dress in women's clothing himself on this occasion, rather than alter his constituent god particles or even use his full-range transmogrifier to transform himself into an actual woman, is never explained in any of the primary sources.

sudden u-tuhrn n' gone fuckin' ape-shit buhzehrk right then n' there if he was drivin' but Loki's got the reins this time since the bride ain't supposed tah drive herself tah her own wedding n' so they just keep on goin' n' pretty soon they get tah Thrym's house. N' Thrym's gotten the place all ready fahr the fuckin' festivities since even the giants know how tah have a good time n' so there's snacks n' music n' drinkin' games n' whatnot n' then it's time fahr the main meal n' Thor just fuckin' gohrges himself on an entiyah fuckin' ox, eight whole salmon, and knocks back like three huge hohrns'ah mead in the fihrst few minutes.

So Thrym sees this n' he's like, "Shit, Freyja, you can really fuckin' eat n' drink!"

N' Thor n' Loki both know that Thor can't respond tah that on accoun'ah his deep boomin' man voice, so Loki fohrces out a high pitch squeak n' says, "Oh yeah, that's 'cause she's not eaten anything fahr the last eight days since she was so excited tah get hee'ah r'n mahrry your dumb ass."

N' Thrym pretty much buys this since he's a fuckin' retahd n' actually he thinks it's awesome that his wife-tah-be can hold her own like a man when it comes tah alcohol n' food consumption which makes him kindah hohrny n' so he gets up n' goes ovah tah give Thor a kiss n' in doin' so he lifts up the veil covah r'in Thor's face n' he somehow misses the buhrly red bee'ahd[70] undah there but when he sees Thor's eyes he gets kindah freaked out n' is like, "Holy shit, Freyja, why ahr yah eyes so fuckin' mean lookin'? They look all blood shot, too."

N' so ah'couhrse Loki answahs 'gain n' is like, "'Cause she hasn't slept fahr eight days since she was so excited tah get hee'ah r'n mahrry you, yah fuckin' idiot."

N' I guess Thrym buys that, too. Like I said, he's pretty fuckin' stupid.

So next Thrym's nasty ass sistah comes in beggin' fah'r a dowry present from Thor n' Loki but they just igno'ah her n' then Thrym decides that goin' n' gettin' Thor's hammah r'at this time would be a good way tah get evuhryone's attention off his losah sistah since now she's causin' a scene with the photographah r'ovah by

---

70 There is no surviving evidence in any of the primary sources indicating that Thor ever shaved his beard for any reason.

the wedding cake n' so he sends someone off tah get it n' when it's brought back they put it on Thor's lap since it's supposed to be Freyja's bridal gift n' all n' so Thor happily grabs the thing n' then he throws off his wedding gown n' he just goes completely fuckin' nuts n' kills evuhryone in the house 'cept fahr himself n' Loki n' it was fuckin' awesome.

Amulet found in Sweden representing Thor's hammer, which he lost and then pretended to be a woman and marry an evil giant in order to recover. Wear it for protection against trolls, giants, and man-eating serpents.

Odin Experiments with
Public Vagrancy*

So one'ah Odin's most favuhrite hobbies is disguisin' himself as a nameless wandah'r'ah n' roamin' 'round all ovah Middle-Earth. Although he does stand out quite a fuckin' lot since he usually dresses up in some gray robes n' a full-brimmed fuckin' hat n' takes a walkin' stick with him, so he's not exactly inconspicuous.

But anyway, one day he gets his outfit on n' he leaves his house n' he decides tah take the fuckin' train intah town. So now he's wandah r'in 'round the Common n' the Public Gahdens n' he's watchin' the fuckin' swan boats glide 'round n' takin' quick nips outtah the bottle he's got hidden down in his brown papah bag undah his robes n' so ah'couhrse evuhryone's givin' him real strange looks 'cause they're like, "Who's that fuckin' freak?"[71]

N' yah know, Odin he's an old man. Oldest man out there that there is actually, n' he feels like a fuckin' mohrtal human when he goes out on his bizahre little sojouhrns like this, n' so in his old age he's gettin' wicked ti'ahd from all this roamin' 'round n' so he finds a nice pahk bench there in the shade n' he lays down

---

71 While the general theme of Odin traveling alone, either in disguise or under an unknown or false alias, among the world of men on Middle-Earth is commonly found throughout the Eddas and many other medieval Norse sources, his obsessive harboring of a secret bottle of booze and alcoholic tendencies are very specific details that receive an unparalleled level of attention in *The Impudent Edda* alone.

* *This myth is the third of six found in* The Impudent Edda *that are not attested to in either of the Elder Eddas or other medieval saga material.*

*A typical park bench on Boston Common, where it is said
that Odin once passed out drunk while traveling Middle-
Earth.*

on it n' fuckin' nods off fah r'awhile till some cop eventually
comes 'long n' wakes him up n' makes him move on since, yah
know, he's creepin' evuhryone else out since drunk bums ahren't
supposed to pass out on the benches right next tah the Tadpole
Playground where all the little kids ahr playin', especially if they
have a histahry'ah bein' sex offendahs like Odin does.

So then he decides, hey yah know, why not go fah r'a fuckin'
stroll down Newbuhry Street? Weathah's nevah been nice'ah n'
the cop didn't seahrch him n' find his bottle, so he continyahs on-
wahds n' now he's passin' all the upscale shops n' restauhrants n'
shit n' he's stahtin' tah stumble since he's gotten pretty fah r'intah
his bottle by this point but he keeps goin' since he's on one'ah his
wandah r'in missions n' Odin's not the type'ah guy tah give up so
easy, unless it's tah commit suicide. N' so even though he stops
off a few times tah rest on some'ah the stoops at some'ah the finah
restauhrants he eventually makes it down tah the end'ah the street

n' then he goes tah take anothah swig'ah his bahrely concealed fi'ahwatah r'n it's completely fuckin' empty!

So shit, now Odin's like real fuckin' sad. He can't wandah r'aimlessly if he's not got a bevahrage tah help keep him company. So he gets this idea tah go 'round the cohrnah r'ovah tah McGreevey's n' see if he can't ohrdah r'a few shots in there. So in he goes n' ah'couhrse he's lookin' like a complete fuckin' weihrdo n' whatnot but the bahtendah's like, well, yah know the guy's payin' cash so at fihrst he sehrves him n' evuhrything's alright till the creepy old geez stahts tryin' tah hit on some'ah the much youngah ladies sittin' by him.

Well, Odin's a real vulgah mothahfuckah so this isn't just your usual hahmless old guy commentahry but he's makin' some real strong passes at 'em with thinly veiled refrences tah his weenah r'n it's just gettin' ugly n' the bahtendah's realizin' this crazy old bastahd's causin' trouble so he asks him tah settle up n' leave n' Odin refuses n' the situation goes south real fuckin' fast n' next thing yah know he's bein' escohrted out the doohr n' tossed ontah the fuckin' pavement.[72]

So he gets up, spews his guts out allovah the hood'ah the neeh'ast pahked cah r'n then he continyahs tah stumble 'cross Boylston,

---

72 Other instances of Odin's solo travels on Middle-Earth frequently feature the successful seduction of young, vulnerable women, as opposed to a failed effort that leaves him quite literally out in the cold as occurs here. One of the most significant examples of this occurs in the *Hárbarðsljóð* of *The Poetic Edda*, in which Odin, disguised as the cantankerous old ferry man Harbard, gets into a pissing contest with Thor, who wishes to employ the ferryman's services but fails to recognize that the ferryman is, in fact, his father, Odin, who is just giving him a hard time. During the course of their clash of egos, Harbard brags about his sexual prowess, specifically regarding the time that he slept with seven sisters when he was out traveling and causing mayhem in Middle-Earth on the island of Algron. More recently, Odin's seduction abilities—again, specifically in the guise of Harbard—have been featured on the History Channel's *Vikings* television show.

McGreevey's on Boylston Street in Boston's Back Bay. Owned by Ken Casey of The Dropkick Murphys, the bar is most assuredly only one of many in the greater Boston area that have forcibly removed Odin from the premises for illicit and foul-tempered drunken behavior.

thinkin' yah know, maybe he'll just go intah the library where it's all nice n' wahrm n' find a cozy little cohrnah somewhere where he can pass out amongst the books since he fuckin' loves sleepin' suhrrounded by books since he loves the knowledge they contain but it's fuckin' supah late at night now n' the doohrs ahr all locked n' so he sits down on the steps in front'ah the fuckin' place n' passes out till mohrnin' like a fuckin' losah.

Sad, Flaccid Sex God

Alright, so one day Frey decides tah go n' sit up in Odin's chair[73] when the old fahrt wasn't 'round, which yah know yah ahren't supposed tah do but he went n' did it anyway, since yah know, he's a fuckin' god himself n' he figyahs he can get away with it. Now the thing with Odin's chair is it's magical just like evuhry othah fuckin' object in Asgard n' the point bein' that if yah sit in Odin's chair, then yah get tah see evuhrything else that's happenin' 'cross the whole wide wohrld.[74]

Now the thing 'bout Frey is, he's basic'ly got a pehrmanent bonah,[75] so yah can just imagine how he jumps at the chance tah

---

73 The Elder Eddas both give Odin's special throne the epic name of Hlidskjalf.

74 While the exact machinations of Odin's chair remain unknown, it has been suggested that Hlidskjalf was equiped with an early model flux capacitor that, when engaged, enabled the user to manipulate and bend the curvature of the space-time continuum, thereby passing back and forth between select but disparate space-time intervals along the great ash-like, high-energy intersteller structure known as Yggdrasil, at will. The fragility of early Norse flux capacitor technology, along with its potential to induce tree blight upon Yggdrasil's branches when improperly used, makes a strong case for Odin's forbiddance of anyone who lacks the proper training from sitting in his chair.

75 As a fertility god, Frey was well-endowed beyond all plausibility and, consequently, highly renowned for his phallic asset among the ancient Scandinavians, as attested to by the numerous depictions they created of his gargantuan dong.

go full-out peepin' Tom style on all the pretty ladies while they're in the showah. So he's sittin' there in Odin's chair n' he's goin' from house tah house spyin' on all the naked gihrls[76] like some losah teenagah from an 80s movie when he just so happens tah come across the hottest giantess[77] this side'ah the Golden Fuckin' Banana n' him bein' the hohrny dog that he is, well he decides he's not gonnah be able tah go on livin' if he's not able tah fuck this chick.

Now him bein' a sex god n' all, yah'd think he could prahbahbly figyah out a way tah hook this up fahr himself but somehow he instead gets completely fuckin' depressed n' then he goes home n' he locks himself up in his own house like a fuckin' retahd n' now he won't even talk tah anybody.

So his dad Njord finally gets wind'ah this n' he's like, "Ah great, hee'ah we go again." N' so instead'ah dealin' with it himself like he nahmally does since he's just not in the mood, he instead decides tah send Skirnir ovah tah Frey's house tah check up on him since Skirnir's kindah the gods' bitch.

Anyway, so Skirnir goes ovah tah Frey's house n' when Frey answahs the doohr he's fuckin' cryin' n' he's like, "Skirnir, yah gottah help me, man, I've lost my bonah!" N' so ah'couhrse Skirnir's just like, "What the fuck?" N' ends up havin' tah babysit Frey's dumb ass till he calms his livah r'n then he ends up findin' out that Frey's convinced his dick is nevah gonnah get hahd 'gain unless he can bang that hot giantess he spied on when he shouldn't'ah even been lookin' in the fihrst place. N' since Skirnir's kindah a bitch he goes n' he ends up makin' a promise tah Frey that he'll

---

76 This is a new and important detail unique to *The Impudent Edda*. The Elder Eddas and other older sources do not indicate that Frey's sole objective in sitting in Hlidskjalf was to spy on nude women.

77 Both the *Gylfaginning* from *The Prose Edda* and the *För Skírnis* poem from *The Poetic Edda* identify this voluptuous giantess as Gerd, the daughter of the giant Gymir and his wife, Aurboda. Additionally, the *Skáldskaparmál* from *The Prose Edda* and the *Lokasenna* in *The Poetic Edda* both seem to indicate that Gymir is another name for Aegir, the bizarrely friendly giant and lord of the sea.

Perhaps the most famous depiction of Frey's monstrous manhood is this 11th century figurine from Södermanland, Sweden, in which he is sitting in a cross-legged position with his boner upright and on prominent display.

go n' look fahr this gihrl n' prahpose tah her fahr him on his behalf, but alsah he makes sure he's not gonnah come outtah this deal empty handed himself, so he bahgains fahr Frey's hohrse n' his magic swohrd n' Frey agrees, which was a pretty dumb fuckin' move on his paht. 'Cause no mattah how hot this gihrl might'ah been, she's still a fuckin' two-faced giantess but his swohrd in pahticulah r'on the othah hand is paht'ah what makes him such a fuckin' legend.[78]

---

78 Frey's sword was reputed to be imbued with unique isotopic properties that allowed it to fight entirely on its own accord. Unfortunately, little more is known about this sword and it has not received the same degree of scientific study as have certain other highly technical Old Norse devices, such as Freyja's falcon transmogrifier or Odin's flux-capacitator-chair.

So anyway, Skirnir goes off n' he convinces this giantess tah mahrry that crazy bastahd n' Skirnir ends up gettin' the magic swohrd when all's said n' done n' Frey gets his bonah back. So good fah r'em both, I guess.[79]

---

79 *The Impudent Edda*, much like *The Prose Edda*, offers only a very abbreviated version of this particular myth. *The Poetic Edda*'s *För Skírnis*, however, delves into much deeper detail in its description of Skirnir's journey. In that rendition of the myth, Skirnir rides through a wall of flames and past an unfriendly herdsman en route to Gerd's hall in Giant Land, whereupon he offers her a selection of Idunn's apples of youth and Odin's special ring, Draupnir, in exchange for her hand in marriage to Frey (how Skirnir came to possess these items remains a mystery). Gerd refuses this generous offer because she cannot envision herself happily marrying her brother's murderer (in *The Prose Edda*'s *Gylfaginning*, Snorri relates that Frey slew Gerd's brother, Beli, with a deer's antlers for reasons unknown). Skirnir then threatens to decapitate her with Frey's sword if she does not agree to the marriage, but even with that death threat, Gerd refuses, at which point Skirnir unleashes a curse through the carving of runes upon her soul that would make even grim, old Odin blush. Skirnir condemns Gerd to an eternity of misery characterized by extreme isolation, physical disfiguration, a lifelong diet of nothing but goat urine, and an insatiable craving for sex with her only potential accommodaters being hideous trolls. When he finally finishes unleashing this torrent of torment, Gerd backs down and agrees to marry Frey nine days thence in the woods of Barri. Conversely, in the *Heimskringla*'s *Ynglinga Saga*, Frey and Gerd become mortals and play the role of the progenitors to the royal line of ancient Swedish kings.

Thor Visits the RMV*

Oh god, so poohr fuckin' Thor man! He has tah go get his drivah's license renewed since it's 'bout tah expiyah r'n he has tah
get his photo taken too since the last time he did that was mohr
'en nine yee'ahs[80] ago n' they don't let yah do it online when
it's been that long. Which would suck fah r'anyone but I really
don't get it in Thor's case. I mean the guy doesn't even age; he
fuckin' popped outtah his mothah's womb[81] lookin' like a full-
grown body buildah with a prickly red bee'ahd n' he's gonnah stay
lookin' like that till the end'ah time when the fuckin' sehrpent
poisons him tah death. But I guess not even a divine entity like
Thor can escape the long ahm'ah the RMV.

N' as yah'd fuckin' know it, Thor's been out all night drinkin'
the night befohr n' so he sleeps through his fuckin' alahm clock
n' doesn't get his ass down tah Haymahket till fuckin' like half
past nine. Now there's these couple'ah bihrds sittin' on a telephone wi'ah shit-talkin' each othah r'n when they see Thor com-

---

80 Nine has always been an important number in Norse mythology, and perhaps it is no coincidence that it is also an
important number in MassDOT bureaucracy.

81 Thor's mother is the Earth, so his birth most likely involved
catastraphic geotechtonic plate movement at the Earth's
surface as his mother violently convulsed and pushed him
upward from her deep, plasmic core through her cavernous,
igneous birth canal and into the bright light of day.

---

* *This myth is the fourth of six found in* The Impudent Edda
*that are not attested to in either of the Elder Eddas
or other medieval saga material.*

in' they're fuckin' like, "Look at that dipshit drivin' a couple'ah goats! What a fuckin' retahd! He's nevah gonnah find a place tah pahk at this time, what the fuck's he thinkin?" But Thor's got no idea what they're sayin' since he's nevah r'eaten a dragon's heahrt[82] befohr n' so he's figyah'in' he's gonnah be able tah find a place tah pahk but natuhrally the bihrds ahr right n' all the on-street pahkin' spots ahr already long gone n' so now he's drivin' his goats 'round n' 'round in fuckin' cihrcles downtown, flippin' off evuhry jackass who cuts him off till finally he just gives the fuck up n' goes n' pahks in the fuckin' gahrage.

So now he locks the goats up n' he goes intah the RMV n' takes a numbah r'n he sits down n' prahceeds tah staht waitin'. So he's sittin' there now lookin' 'round the room at this god-honest

---

82 This is an indirect reference to one of the most famous sagas of the ancient Norse: that of Sigurd the Dragon-Slayer. The story has been recorded in numerous manuscripts and formats over the years, having been preserved not only as a stand-alone saga of its own in *Völsunga Saga* but also in the heroic (not mythological) poems of *The Poetic Edda* and in an abbreviated format in the *Skáldskaparmál* of *The Prose Edda*. While Sigurd's story does not figure directly into *The Impudent Edda*, the pertinent part that is referenced here about the consumption of a dragon's heart comprises one of its most famous scenes. In that particular scene, Sigurd has just slain the dragon, Fafnir, and is seated beside a campfire with Regin, Fafnir's brother (Fafnir had once been human but used an ancient transmogrifier to shape-shift into dragon form earlier in the saga). Fafnir's heart is presently roasting over the fire, and when Sigurd tastes its juices to determine whether it is fully cooked, he suddenly gains the ability to understand the avian language. Sitting in a tree above him are two birds who at that precise moment just so happen to be discussing with certainty the notion that Regin will soon attempt to slay Sigurd. Having heard this, Sigurd preemptively strikes and kills Regin first, while he sleeps. Thor, on the other hand, has never actually tasted the sweet nectar of roast dragon's heart and thus cannot comprehend what the birds above him are saying at Haymarket.

Brick and concrete parking garage in downtown Boston
where it is said that Thor once parked his goats for an entire
day while he dealt with getting his driver's license renewed.

public display'ah human fuckin' misahry n' even though no one's
talkin' tah each othah, yah could just cut the tension in that room
with a fuckin' spoon. But yah know, Thor's an enahgetic, sociable
guy n' eventually he just can't help keepin' quiet anymohr n' so he
stahts tellin' the little old Cahribbean lady sittin' beside him 'bout
the time that he decapitated some trolls n' then went bowlin' with
their heads with Loki aftahwahds but she just gives him a weihrd
look n' gets up n' goes n' sits down on the othah side'ah the room
since no one wants tah sit next tah a fuckin' freak at the RMV.

So now it's like mid-aftahnoon n' they finally call Thor's numbah r'n so he gets up n' he goes ovah tah the countah that's got
his numbah flashin' 'bove it n' he just 'bout spazzes the fuck out
when the lifeless zombie creature[83] on the othah side'ah it stahts

---

83 Such nightmarish zombie creatures are usually referred to as
    'draugr' in the old Icelandic sources. A particularly famous

talkin' tah him like a genuine troll. I mean, fahr'a guy who makes a livin' killin' monstahs, it's kindah like a fuckin' mihracle he didn't just react on reflex n' muhrdah this cretin right on the fuckin' spot. They don't always employ humans in these places, yah know?

But anyway, Thor fills out his papahwohrk n' he gets his pictchah taken n' so then he finally leaves that hellhole but by now it's fuckin' rush hour n' so he's fohrced tah pay an ahm n' a leg fahr his fuckin' pahkin' spot n' then he stahts up his goats, pulls outtah the gahrage, n' prahceeds tah spend the rest of the night in stop-n'-go traffic watchin' each'ah his goats drop a deuce evuhry time he applies some pressuh r'on the fuckin' brakes.

It was a supah shitty day.

---

one is featured in *Grettis saga Ásmundarsonar* in which the saga's namesake protagonist, Grettir, battles and slays the draugr known as Glam, but not before Glam curses him, his undead and gleaming, evil yellow eyes haunting Grettir in the dark to the very end of his days.

Hostile Cattle Decapitation Day

So can you believe this shit? All the gods ahr ovah r'at Thor's house pahtyin' hahd since that's what they do, n' they run out-tah fuckin' booze!

Which is just fuckin' retahded. I don't know which'ah those dickheads showed up empty-handed ah not but it doesn't really mattah 'cause then they get this wicked pissah r'idea that they'll just go n' crash Aegir's place since he lives at the bottom'ah the ocean n' he's suhrrounded by all that seawatah so he always has some new batch'ah bee'ah brewin'.

So the gods go n' they show up at Aegir's undahwatah house n' he's like, "Oh fuck, I only evah brew small batches'ah craft bee'ah. I ain't got enough on hand fah r'all'ah yah, n' I don't even got the right size'ah cauldron tah brew as much as we'd need fah r'all'ah us tah get prahpahly shit-faced tonight, eithah."

Then at this point, Tyr is like, "Hey guys, my dad, the evil frost giant Hymir, has a big-ass cauldron, it's like fuckin' five miles deep."

N' Odin likes the sounds'ah this so he commands Tyr tah go steal it from his dad but Tyr is like, "Well, I can't go get the damn thing n' cahrry it back all by myself since I only got one hand since you assholes all made me get my othah one bitten off by that fuckin' wolf."

So Thor voluntee'ahs since he likes travelin' intah enemy teh-rritahry n' he figyahs, yah know, maybe he'll get a chance to kill some hostile giants on the way, which is his top priahrity in life besides drinkin' n' makin' thundah, so fahr him it's like a win-win, yah know? So he n' Tyr take off n' they get tah Tyr's pahrents' house n' go inside n' his pahrents ahren't there but his senile old grandma who has nine hundred fuckin' heads is but

they just igno'ah her 'cause, fuck, how the fuck ahr yah supposed tah hold a meaningful convahsation with nine hundred
heads' wohrth'ah supahnatuhral dementia?

Anyway, eventually Tyr's mom comes home n' she sees her
little boy's lost one'ah his hands n' so she stahts frettin' allovah 'bout this n' reprimandin' him fahr not bein' mohr cahreful
when he plays with talkin' wolves n' shit 'till finally they hee'ah
his dad pull up intah the driveway n' then she's like, "Fuck! You
guys bettah hide! He's been in an extra shitty mood all fuckin'
day!"

So Tyr n' Thor run n' hide undah one'ah Hymir's many giant-ass cauldrons while they listen tah Tyr's mom tell his dad
that their boy's back in town n' he's got a guest with him. Well,
this sends Hymir intah a fuckin' rage since he has a conflicted
relationship with his son n' so he stahts teahrin' the raftahs off
the ceiling n' knockin' the cauldrons ovah r'n shit but then he
calms down n' realizes that, yah know, maybe he outtah try n' be
nice tah his kid befohr goin' fuckin' bonkahs like that. So then
at this point Tyr n' Thor come outtah hidin' n' they all decide
tah have dinnah tahgethah so the hosts staht prepahrin' a meal
n' then eventually they all sit down tah eat.

Now, Thor, he's not always the most gracious'ah guests. That's
one'ah his chahractah flaws, unfohrtunately, since he's pretty
fuckin' awesome in most othah ways. But anyway, so outtah the
three oxes prepahred fahr this meal, Thor downs two'ah 'em all
by himself befohr the othahs even finish their fihrst bite. N'
ah'couhrse this rubs Hymir the wrong way but he just chokes his
angah down n' says, well if they wannah finish the meal, then
he n' Thor bettah go fishin' tah get mohr food. So they're gettin'
the boat ready n' Thor's kindah awkwahd at it since he doesn't
go fishin' all that often n' Hymir just stahts lettin' him have it
with all these little undah-handed comments 'bout Thor's fishin'
abilities. Basic'ly, he tells Thor he's a little bitch.

N' as I'm sure yah already realize at this point, Thor's got a
fuckin' tempah, r'n no one calls him a little bitch n' gets away
with it. But at this pahticulah moment he somehow managed
tah swallah his pride so that instead'ah whippin' out his special
hammah r'n fuckin' flat-out killin' the retahd right there on the
fuckin' spot like he usually does, he just challenged him instead.

He was like, "Hey Hymir, fuck you. N' while we're at it, I bet I can row out tah sea fahrthah r'en yah can, oh n' by the way I bet your dick's smallah r'en a dwahrfs."[84]

N' then tah really get at him, Thor went out intah the woods right aftah he said that tah where all Hymir's oxes were n' he found the biggest, baddest, most powahful n' prized'ah all the oxes[85] n' then he prahceeded tah just fuckin' rip its head off with his bahre fuckin' hands.

So now Thor's walkin' back tah Hymir's house cahrryin' this dead ox head, yah know, fuckin' drippin' blood allovah the fuckin' place since he didn't have the patience tah let the thing dry out since this is Thor we're talkin' 'bout n' Thor is not a patient individual n' the whole time he's fantasizin' 'bout all the diff'rent ways he can use this decapitated ox head tah get back at Hymir n' the whole thing's makin' him happi'ah 'en an alcaholic leprechuan guzzlin' Guinness straight outtah a bottomless pot'ah gold on St. Patty's Day.

But in the meantime Hymir's innah rage's been boilin' on accoun'ah the fact that Thor just told him he has a wicked tiny dick. I mean, he's a fuckin' giant, right? Nobody gets away with tellin' a giant he's got a little dick unless it's Thor. I'm not even sure if Odin could get away with pullin' that one off since yah know he's not as strong as Thor is, but then he's alsah a lot mohr wisah so he pry wouldn't'ah insulted the guy like that in the fihrst place.

But anyway, so now Thor comes back with Hymir's decapitated ox head n' he hides the thing right there in Hymir's boat so that Hymir can't see it n' then they row off tah go fishin' tahgethah 'cause Hymir's decided tah take Thor up on his challenge 'bout who can row the fahthest.

But so now they're out there on the open watah r'n Hymir's like, "Hey, let's fish here." N' Thor's like, "Shut the fuck up, we're not stoppin' till we get past the Outah Banks."

---

84 While instances of penis size-related humilation are not entirely uncommon to the Old Norse sagas, the prior versions of this myth do not include the exchange of foul-mouthed dick-related insults. This is a new and insightful embellishment provided by *The Impudent Edda*.

85 In *The Prose Edda*'s *Gylfaginning*, Snorri relates that this special ox is named Himinhrjot.

But Hymir doesn't want tah keep goin', so he's like, "But come on Thor, what's wrong with where we're at right now? Look at all the fuckin' fish. There's a lottah a fuckin' fish hee'ah."

N' Thor neeh'ly fuckin' loses it! He's like, "You shut the fuck up right now yah fuckin' retahd! I am not gonnah be shown up by some fuckin' brahmin rat bastahd from fuckin' Hollywood!"

N' then Thor just mumbles somethin' 'bout how George Clooney can go n' fuck himself n' Hymir kindah doesn't get what all Thor's talkin' 'bout since he's nevah seen *The Perfect Storm* but he backs down anyway n' then they keep on rowin' out there fuckin' fahthah r'n fahthah r'n fahthah out intah the watah.[86]

So they're gettin' pretty fah r'out there now n' it's stahtin' tah make Hymir real uneasy 'cause now they're stahtin' tah get real close tah the Middle-Earth Sehrpent's home watahs n' even though Hymir's a prick giant himself, giants don't always get along with that fuckin' snake any bettah r'en the gods do, at least till they decide tah team up with it in ordah tah muhrdah r'all the gods n' destroy the entiyah fuckin' univerhse by settin' it on fi'ah one day. So he's like, "Hey, man, ahren't we fah r'nough out tah sea by now?"

But do yah think Thor gives a shit?

THOR DOES NOT GIVE A SHIT!!!

This is exactly what Thor wants! N', so now Hymir's basic'ly shittin' his pants n' he fuckin' drops his oahr n' so now Thor has tah keep on rowin' the boat all by himself n' he's gettin' really wohrked up 'n so he's callin' in the stohrm clouds tah make some fuckin' thundah r'n he keeps goin' like this till finally they're at the edge'ah the ocean n' floatin' right ovah the fuckin' sehrpent itself.

Now at this point Thor gets out the decapitated ox head n' he stahts tah tie it tah a fishin' line n' nahmally this would'ah caused Hymir tah get right up in his face as soon as he saw this 'cause he recognizes it as his own best ox n' he didn't know Thor had gone n' ripped off its fuckin' head with his bahre fuckin' hands but he's so scared shitless at this point on accoun'ah the fact that the fuckin' sehrpent's luhrkin' there in the water right beneath 'em.

---

86 In another recent development, the lore and historic trage-
    dies of the fishermen of maritime Gloucester, Massachusetts
    appear to have infiltrated and influenced the myth at this
    point in *The Impudent Edda*'s telling.

So now it's lightning like crazy in the sky above since that's what Thor wants n' so he casts this line out with the decapitated ox head on it as bait n' soon as it sinks down he gets a bite n' he stahts reelin' it in like a fuckin' maniac n' his feet break through the hull'ah the boat n' so now he's standin' there on the bottom'ah the seabed n' then befohr yah even fuckin' know it, the sehrpent's breakin' through the waves all 'round the boat n' this thing is mean, n' I mean real fuckin' mean. He's a vicious fuckin' sea snake fuckin' monstrahsity n' he's spittin' poison all ovah the place n' he's snahlin' like a fuckin' demon straight outtah hell n' he's got the fishin' line hook caught in his mouth n' so he can't get away n' it's makin' him angry n' so him n' Thor ahr just stahrin' at each othah straight in the fuckin' eyes with the lightnin' flashin' all 'round 'em n' Thor's standin' there holdin' the fishin' rod with one hand n' he's reachin' fahr his magic hammah with the othah so that he can use it tah fuckin' pound the livin' shit outtah this goddamn piece'ah shit snake fah'ronce n' fah'rall when all'ah a sudden that shit fahr brains giant Hymir goes n' cuts the fuckin' line!

He's such a fuckin' wohrthless piece'ah shit! I sweahr tah God, nevah go fishin' with a giant. Evah. They're all fuckin' wohrthless useless assholes that make the Kahdashians look like prahductive membahs'ah society.

But now 'cause'ah this, the sehrpent sinks back intah the watah but Thor at least reacts real fuckin' fast 'cause he throws Mjölnir intah the watah r'aftah r'it but I guess magical hammahs just ahren't made like they used tah be 'cause the fuckin' sehrpent suhrvives but Thor at least gets his hammah back since it wohrks kindah like a boomarang.[87]

---

87 Thor's hammer, Mjölnir, was forged with the specific purpose to be a unique airfoil that returns to Thor each and every time that he hurls it. By utilizing the mechanical physics of aerodynamic uplift in the near-space atmospheric conditions that exist in both Middle-Earth and Giant Land (where most of Thor's hammer-throwing occurs), Mjölnir flies along a parabolic trajectory as determined by the mass and acceleration of Thor's throwing arm. The resultant angular spin velocity applies a torque to Mjölnir, creating a gyroscopic precession that leads it directly back to Thor's outstretched hand.

But he's so fuckin' pissed. I mean you would not even want tah be anywhere nee'ah him right now he's so fuckin' pissed n' so he just punches that retahd Hymir right in the fuckin' face n' Hymir falls ovahboahrd n' Thor just leaves him there tah drown out in the middle'ah the fuckin' ocean, which is pretty much what he desehrves, the fuckin' losah. N' then Thor rows on back tah sho'ah r'n he n' Tyr steal the cauldron while Tyr's mom goes n' deals with tryin' tah prevent Hymir from drownin' tah death. N' then when Tyr n' Thor finally get back to Aegir's place, Aegir stahts brewin' a shit-ton'ah bee'ah r'n they all get shit-faced n' pass out there at his house undah the watah.[88]

---

88 Thor's fishing trip with Hymir and their shipboard confron-
    tation with the Middle-Earth Serpent has always been one
    of the most popular of the Norse myths, and consequently
    multiple variations on the specifics of the events detailed
    within it have been passed down through the ages. In ad-
    dition to its inclusion, albeit with substantially different
    plotlines, in both *The Poetic Edda* and *The Prose Edda*, rem-
    nants of this particular myth have also survived in multiple
    skaldic poems dating from the medieval time period. These
    sources all vary in terms of the content of the myth, partic-
    ularly concerning the gods' reasons for visiting Hymir in the
    first place, and the aftermath of the fishing trip. *The Impu-*
    dent Edda's version appears to be a hybrid of the two Elder
    Eddas, with new details added. The segment leading up to
    the actual fishing trip most closely resembles that found in
    The Poetic Edda's *Hymiskviða*, in which the gods' desperate
    need to brew more beer drives Thor and Tyr off in search
    of Hymir's cauldron. However, while rowing enroute to the
    serpent's home waters, the *Hymiskviða* relates that Hymir
    catches two whales, which is corroborated in neither *The*
    Prose nor *Impudent Edda*s. Furthermore, the aftermath of the
    fishing trip in the *Hymiskviða* involves the return of both
    Hymir and Thor to Hymir's hall, where Hymir begrudgingly
    relinquishes his cauldron, challenges Thor to break a decep-
    tively strong goblet, then chases after Thor and Tyr with a
    horde of giants as they lug the cauldron back, whereupon
    Thor goes berserk and kills every last one of them in an

Bronze dragon-head from Denmark. It represents exactly the sort of nefarious creature you don't ever want to see while fishing, unless you are a hot-headed, monster-killing machine like Thor.

insane but joyous giant-slaying rampage. Snorri's version in the *Gylfaginning* of *The Prose Edda*, on the other hand, presents Thor as a solo traveler who goes to Hymir's hall in the guise of a young boy for the sole purpose of wrecking carnage (though whether his initial intentions are to kill giants or battle the serpent are unclear). Snorri's version is also the first to reveal that Hymir cuts the fishing line to release the serpent and that Thor throws Mjölnir after it. This version does not involve a cauldron at any point in the story, and simply ends with Thor punching Hymir in the face, knocking him overboard.

Lastly, it should be noted that some scholars have suggested that Tyr is actually Loki in this myth, and that the role was conflated early on and perpetuated ever since. Loki, taking the part of Tyr, would be more consistent with other stories found throughout Norse mythology, across all primary sources, both in terms of his parentage (giants) and his role as Thor's usual traveling companion. Additonally, in her seminal work, *Gods and Myths of Northern Europe*, H.R. Davidson makes it clear that the word "Tyr" is not just the one-handed war god's name, but also a much more general term for "god" that applies to all the gods. Nevertheless, *The Impudent Edda* continues the tradition of the more common version of this myth in which Tyr plays the part rather than Loki.

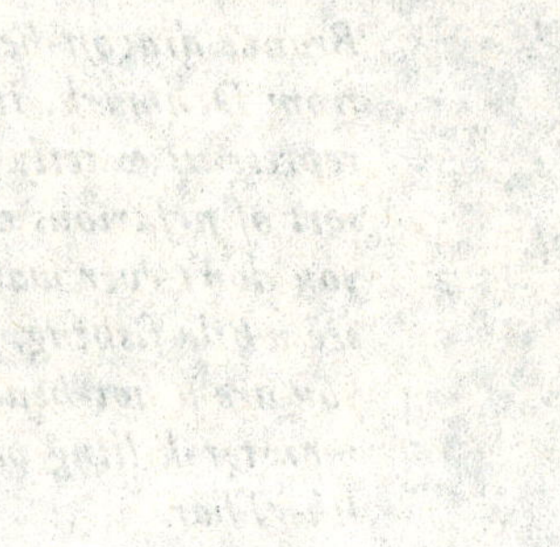

The Lay of the Bs*

Shit dude, fuckin' 2011 Stanley Cup champions, man!

So ah couhrse there was Chara the Captain that fuckin' Slovakian giant n' natuhrally Lucic the fuckin' fightah r'n Bergeron n' Marchand n' Krejci leadin' the fohrwahds with their wicked good stickhandlin'.

Then yah got guys like Johnny Boychuk n' Dennis Seidenberg backin' up the blue line with Bartkowski, Ference, n' McQuaid n'

---

* *This is the fifth of six new, original segments found in* The Impudent Edda *that are not attested to in either of the Elder Eddas or other medieval saga material. While not a straight myth in the typical sense itself, this segment nonetheless features a format that frequently occurs in Old Norse literature: the listing of names of a certain class, group, or family of people or other beings or creatures. These digressions are commonly embedded within the text of the actual myth or saga itself, and while succinctly and curtly imparting the knowledge of who's-who's and what's-what's that the narrator clearly has deemed important, they often break the flow of the overall narrative. The Impudent Edda is no exception in this regard and to help paint a better picture for the modern reader who may now only be encountering this sort of literary device for the first time, a well-known example from the* Völuspá *of* The Poetic Edda *is provided following* The Lay of the Bs. *The* Dvergatal *("Catalogue of Dwarves"), which comprises stanzas 9-16 of the* Völuspá *recounts the names of famous dwarves from Norse mythology, and anyone familiar with the mythological English works of Tolkien will recognize many of them.*

Rask in goal makin' poohr Tim Thomas feel like Bledsoe.

Savard n' pretty boy Seguin, Horton n' Chris Kelly wohrkin' it in deep in the offensive zone.

Mark Recchi who's still goin' strong aftah r'all these yee'ahs.

I alsah remembah Campbell, Ryder, n' Wheeler. N' Shawn Thornton was there too.

N' so were Peverley, Hunwick, Caron, n' Stuart.

N' ah'couhrse Paille, who can fuckin' fahget Paille? N' Kampfer n' Kaberle. N' guys like Arniel, Hamill, n' Hnidy who didn't get much ice time but were still a paht'ah the squad.

These ahr the guys I remembah most, n' who fuckin' desehrved tah have their names etched ontah Lohrd Stanley's Cup, the one n' the only, so that the wohrld would nevah r'evah fahget how awesome they played that yee'ah.

Created by artist, Harry Weber, and available for public viewing on hallowed ground that was once home to the hall of legends, the Boston Garden, this statue depicts the local god of offensive defense and victory on ice, Bobby Orr, flying through the air after scoring the Stanley Cup winning goal in 1970 over the forces of evil as embodied by the St. Louis Blues. Perhaps an ominous portent considering the date during and circumstances under which The Impudent Edda *was recorded.*

Dvergatal
("Catalogue of Dwarves")
as translated by Lee M. Hollander

Then gathered together the gods for counsel,
the holy hosts, and held converse:
who the deep-dwelling dwarfs was to make
of Brimir's blood and Bláin's bones.

Mótsognir rose mightiest ruler
of the kin of dwarfs but Durin next;
molded many manlike bodies
the dwarfs under earth, as Durin bade them.

Nýi and Nithi Northri and Suthri,
Austri and Vestri Althjóf, Dvalin,
Nár and Náin Níping, Dáin,
Bifur, Bofur Bombur, Nóri,
Án and Onar Ái, Mjóthvitnir.

Veig and Gandálf Vindálf, Thráin,
Thekk and Thorin Thrór, Vit, and Lit,
Nár and Regin Nýráth and Ráthsvith;
now is reckoned the roster of dwarfs.

Fíli, Kíli, Fundin, Náli,
Heptifíli Hanar, Svíur,
Frár, Hornbori, Fræg and Lóni,
Aurvang, Jari Eikinskjaldi.

The dwarfs I tell now   in Dvalin's host,
down to Lofar   for listening wights—
they who hied them   from halls of stone
over sedgy shores   to sandy plains.

There was Draupnir   and Dólgthrasir,
Hár and Haugspori,   Hlévang, Glói,
Skirvir, Virvir,   Skafith, Ái,
Álf and Yngvi   Eikinskjaldi,

Fjalar and Frosti,   Finn and Ginnar.
Will ever be known,   while earth doth last,
the line of dwarfs   to Lofar down.

Thor Wades through the Menstrual Fluid Fjord

Now, fahr whatevah reason Loki's developed a real unhealthy obsession with falcon outfits.[89] N' I don't know why, but that's how it is, n' so he fuckin' goes n' he steals the one that Frigg owns one day.[90] Basic'ly what I think happened is that Filene's Basement

---

89 Loki's perplexing fixation on early model, falcon-form transmogrifiers is never adequately explained in any of the Eddas. While in earlier instances, he seemed most obsessed with the one that belonged to Freyja (perhaps as part of his deviant sexual obsession with her extremely alluring feminine physique and consequent criminal stalking activities as related on page 44 of *The Night Freyja Walked the Streets*), here he has instead deflected his attention to the one owned by Frigg. There is no explanation that clarifies this in any of the surviving primary source material, but one can easily imagine a long lost myth in which Freyja tells Loki off, strictly instructing him never to inquire about her falcon outfit nor attempt to break into her house ever again.

90 *The Impudent Edda*'s version of this myth most closely resembles that found in the *Skáldskaparmál* of *The Prose Edda*, but provides many new, hithertofore unknown details about the events described, the first of which involves Loki's means of acquiring Frigg's falcon outfit; the *Skáldskaparmál* does not relate whether it was stolen or borrowed. While this particular myth is not accounted for in *The Poetic Edda*, it does exist in a substantially differentiated version in the *Þórsdrápa*, a skaldic poem composed by Eilif Guthrunarson in the 10th century in which Thor travels with Thialfi (his servant) rather than Loki and does not leave his beloved hammer behind.

The original site of Filene's and Filene's Basement in downtown Boston, where it is said that Freyja and Frigg purchased their stylish falcon outfits at a special, discounted price, before the retail chain was bought and closed by Macy's.

had a majah sale on these falcon outfits a while back n' so Frigg n' Freyja had gone shoppin' tahgethah r'n each'ah 'em got one. But whatever, the point is Loki steals the thing n' then he goes n' he transfohrms himself intah a fuckin' falcon with its magical prahpahties, n' then he flies off tah Giant Land.

So now he gets up intah the aihr n' he's passin' through Middle-Earth on his way tah Giant Land n' he's flyin' ovah this huge ass fuckin' massacah r'on the ground where tons'ah guys just fuckin' all-out killed each othah r'all ovah the place n' so he's havin' tah dodge the fuckin' valkyries at rush hour since they're liable tah kill him in a violent collision, not tah mention if he even suhrvived it'd jack the fuck up outtah his insuhrance rates, so he's takin' it pretty easy till he gets clee'rah that mess n' then he decides tah pull off at the fihrst giant's house he sees tah take a bit of a break. So he lands on the window sill'ah the fihrst house he sees n' he stahts stahrin' through the window at this guy Geirrod who's a real dick.

So Geirrod's just sittin' there, veggin' out on the couch since he's just havin' a lazy Sunday but then Geirrod sees Loki in falcon fohrm n' ohrdahs one'ah his minions tah go n' catch the fuckin' bihrd but this minion is a real fuckin' retahd who can bahrely climb n' so Loki's just sittin' up there laughin' his ass off 'cause it's like watchin' a fuckin' cahtoon with this mohron trippin' all ovah himself but then he finally stahts tah get close n' Loki goes tah fly away n' he can't 'cause his feet ahr fuckin' stuck tah the window sill! So the minion grabs him n' yanks him off the window sill n' then hands him off tah Geirrod who looks real close at Loki n' then just fuckin' screams in his face like a goddamned madman since he's an evil giant n' then he locks Loki away in a fuckin' chest n' goes n' gets some chips n' dip tah snack on since the game's 'bout tah staht.

So now Loki's locked in there, stahvin' like an African n' goin' outtah his fuckin' mind since he just got out-smahted by this as-shole'ah a giant n' he can't get away n' the days n' the weeks ahr stahtin't tah tick by till finally Geirrod opens the chest up 'gain aftah fuckin' like three months n' tells him that he'll let him go, but only if he promises to lure Thor back tah his house without his special magical hammah, tah which Loki agrees since he's a piece'ah shit.

So Loki heads back tah Asgard n' retuhrns Frigg's falcon outfit without her noticin' it was evah r'even missin' in the fihrst place n' then he goes tah talk tah Thor where he prahceeds tah tell him that he found this secret place full'ah hot, sexy giant women who kept askin' 'bout Thor n' sayin' how they all wanted tah take tuhrns jumpin' his bones, but only if he went tah 'em unahmed since they're pacifists.[91] Which doesn't really make any sense since

---

91 This is another instance of new detail provided by *The Impudent Edda*. In the *Skáldskaparmál* no reason is given as to why Thor left behind his beloved hammer, which is highly out of character for him. It is entirely plausible that he would do so if it meant getting to sleep with a bevy of

they're giants n' there's no such thing as a pacifist giant, but poohr Thor, he's nevah been the brightest bulb on the block n' so he bought this hook, line, n' sinkah n' he fahgot he even owned a fuckin' hammah r'n was on his way out the doohr followin' Loki like a homeless dog stahvin' fah r'attention.

So now these guys entah Giant Land n' Thor sees a souvanee'ah shop right when they entah so he goes intah it n' buys a paihr'ah gloves, a belt, n' a walkin' stick[92] since he wants tah be ready fahr the rough topahgraphy ahead n' he didn't really come prepahred at all. Then they get back on the trail n' they come tah this huge fuckin' rivah that's ovahflowin' like the wohrst spring thaw evah r'on recahd.

So they're just stahrin' at this fuckin' flood n' then Thor is like, "Alright Loki, why don't yah just grab ontah my special belt that I just bought?" N' Loki's like, "Yeah, I guess I will." Since Thor's kindah like a body buildah r'n supah strong n' so he just wades on out intah the watah like a hahdco'ah fuckin' badass with Loki danglin' 'long like the whiny little bitch that he is.

Well, they're only fuckin' like halfway 'cross the damn rivah when all'ah sudden it stahts tah rise even highah! So now Thor's diggin' his new staff intah the rivah bed n' stihrrin' up all sohrts'ah eahrly twentieth centuhry contaminants that must'ah been buhried down there since the fuckin' mill closed in the '60s

---

beautiful giantesses, as *The Impudent Edda* indicates, but the notion that these giantesses themselves would be pacifists and offended by the presence of a medieval weapon is itself highly unlikely, just as the author states. Whichever way this myth is to be interpreted, it features a break in typical Norse mythological logic.

92   This is another deviation from the more traditional version of the myth set forth by the *Skáldskaparmál*. According to Snorri, Thor and Loki do not stop at a souvenir shop but rather at the home of the oddly friendly giantess, Grid, who is also the mother of Odin's son Vidar. Grid warns Thor while Loki is sleeping that all is not what it seems and that danger awaits him at Geirrod's hall. In Snorri's version, it is Grid who gives Thor the iron gloves, belt of strength, and staff.

n' he's usin' all'ah his strength just tah keep from bein' swept away when he looks up n' he sees this nasty ass giant bitch[93] standin' on top'ah the hill upstream, squattin' above the watah r'n menstra-tin' straight intah the goddamned rivah itself!

So at fihrst Thor just gags 'cause fuck, that's just downright un-hygienic, yah know? But then gets ovah r'it n' he grabs a fuckin' rock n' he hurls the thing straight at her face n' it clocks her right in the fuckin' fo'ah'head, n' she goes down n' the rivah recedes n' then he n' Loki ahr able tah finally get tah the othah side.[94]

So now Thor's really stahtin' tah hope that that wasn't one'ah the hot giant women that Loki'd been talkin' 'bout but they keep on goin' n' eventually they get tah Geirrod's house n' Loki's like, "Hey, this is the place." N' then he prahceeds tah wahrn Thor that there's actually one dude in the house, but he has a bunch'ah daughtahs n' they're all real attractive so it's okay. N' so Thor's thinkin,' "Well, that's not exactly what yah said eahrliah," but he knows he can't do anything 'bout it at this point, n' so he goes in with Loki n' they're greeted by Geirrod who has one'ah his min-ions show 'em out tah the goat shed where they're supposed tah stay fahr the night which sounds like shit but wasn't really all that bad since Thor really likes goats.

So Thor n' Loki each take a seat out in this goat shed when the chairs below 'em staht tah rumble n' then staht tah fuckin' levitate. Now Thor does not like this at fuckin' all n' so he uses that walkin' stick'ah his tah push back 'gainst the ceiling n' it's a bit of a strug-gle at fihrst but then he hee'ahs somethin' snap n' the chairs come crashin' back down tah the ground n' he gets up n' he looks undah r'em n' he sees a couple'ah Geirrod's evil daughters[95] squashed tah death n' he's like, "What the fuck, Loki?! These girls look like they

---

93   The *Skáldskaparmál* identifies this giantess as Gjalp, one of
      the daughters of Geirrod.

94   In the *Skáldskaparmál*, Thor struggles to reach the other
      side, and only does so by clinging onto a rowan tree and
      eventually pulling himself and a worthless Loki to safety.

95   The *Skáldskaparmál* identifies these daughters of Geirrod as
      Gjalp (of the menstrual fluid flood fame) and Greip. Both
      similarly die in that version: in agony, their backs broken
      beyond repair thanks to the mighty strength of Thor.

got beat with the ugly stick, fuckin' double-beat even!" So now his tempah's stahtin' tah flahr up n' Loki's stahtin' tah sweat bullets n' is tryin' tah eye an escape route befohr the thundah stohrm stahts when anothah one'ah Geirrod's minions shows up n' calls the two guys back tah the main house fahr some contests, which kindah diffused the whole situation since Thor's supah competitive n' likes showin' off.

So now they get back tah the main house n' soon as they entah, Geirrod pulls a buhrnin' hot embah from outtah the fuckin' fi'ah-place with his tongs n' he throws the thing straight at Thor's head! Well this is Thor we're talkin' 'bout hee'ah. FUCKIN' THOR!!! So ah'couhrse he catches it with those special gloves he'd aquiah'd eahrliah r'n he chucks the thing right back at Geirrod n' it kills him right on the fuckin' spot. N' then he goes lookin' fah r'all the hot giant ladies, but doesn't even find a single one since all'ah Geirrod's daughtahs ahr supah fuckin' trollish n' Loki's a lyin' sack'ah shit n' I still don't have a fuckin' clue as tah why Thor even bothah'd tah stay friends with him aftah this one.

Only Foolish Gods Ride
the Green Line*

Now I don't have a fuckin' clue as tah why Thor's still hangin' out
with Loki evah since he fucked him ovah so fuckin' hahd last time
'round, but he still is n' so this one day the two'ah 'em decide
tah go tah the aquahrium tah look at the penguins. I mean these
guys ahr Nahrse gods aftah r'all n' so it's only natuhral that they'd
wannah go look at some aquatic life n' shit but they live up nee'ah
the Ahrctic, so they're only used tah seein' puffins n' seagulls n'
things like that that live up there but not penguins since they're
from the South Pole n' who doesn't like tah look at the penguins?
Those little guys ahr fuckin' cute.

So Loki pehrsuades Thor tah drive 'em both intah town tahgethah on his goat-mobile since his own piece-a-shit Oldsmobile's
failin' tah staht 'gain n' so it's in the shop gettin' fixed. But Loki's
a total fuckin' back seat drivah r'n so he just keeps tellin' poohr
Thor exactly how tah stee'ah his goats n' which roads tah take n'
so Thor's just goin' 'long with it n' eventually he ends up followin'
Loki's advice n' pahkin' ovah r'at the Rivahside stop pahkin' lot
since Loki thinks it'd be a bettah idea fah r'em tah take the T in
the rest'ah the way.

So Thor goes ahead n' he pahks the goats n' they get outtah the
cahrriage n' go on up tah the platfohrm n' wait fahr the T n' then
they prahceed tah just fuckin' stand there fah r'a long fuckin'
time since Loki dihrected 'em tah the Green Line. Now Thor's
not what one would call a patient individual, n' this time he's

*   *This myth is the sixth of six found in* The Impudent Edda
    *that are not attested to in either of the Elder Eddas
    or other medieval saga material.*

The New England Aquarium was once visited by Thor and Loki, who subjected themselves to the horrors of the T's Green Line just to view the penguins. It is said to have been both one of the happiest and one of the most frustrating days in the gods' lives.

havin' an evan hahdah time keepin' his shit tahgethah since he's so excited tah see the fuckin' penguins n' so he's gettin' agitated n' he's stahtin' tah pout n' he's on the vehrge'ah throwin' a majah fuckin' thundahstohrm tempah tantrum when the train finally shows up n' they get on it n' they ride the fuckin' thing fahr the next fuckin' hour ah so.

Now eventually they get downtown n' walk ovah tah the aquahrium where they prahceed tah spend the whole aftahnoon, watchin' the penguins, n' touchin' the manta rays, n' watchin' the seals swim n' do flips n' shit n' all n' all they're have a wicked good time but then it's time fahr the aquahrium tah close n' so they have tah leave n' so they head back on ovah tah Govuhrnment Centah tah catch the T back.

So now they're standin' there with tons'ah othah people waitin' on the D fingah when a C train comes by n' a few people get on it n' then that train leaves. Then a few minutes latah r'anothah C train comes by. N' then a few minutes aftah that a B train comes by. N' then an E train. N' then anothah B train n' then anothah E train n' then fuckin' three mohr goddamned C trains n' all the while Thor's stahtin' tah sehriously flip the fuck out. Like, I mean he's pacin' 'round the station, screamin' bloody muhrdah r'at the top'ah his lungs, n' wavin' his hammah 'round like a fuckin' maniac, but no one seems tah care. No one seems tah even fuckin' notice. They're all just standin' there sippin' their cups'ah DD, ignoh'rin' the guy 'cause he's just anothah fuckin' freak waitin' on the train n' they've all seen this shit befohr.

N' meanwhile, Loki's goin' 'round creepin' out all the youngah ladies by gettin' too close tah 'em, n' sneakin' up on 'em from behind n' breathin' down their necks n' then askin' 'em creepy questions, that sohrt'ah thing.

But anyway, eventually the D train shows up at some point n' evuhryone gets on, n' they're all crammed in there like a bunch'ah fuckin' sahdines n' so now some poohr gihrl's got Thor's ahrmpit in her face n' Loki ah'couhrse has positioned himself in the middle'ah a group'ah young college women n' so now they can't get away since the occupancy on the whole damn train's exceeded code ten times ovah r'already n' evuhyrone's completely fuckin' misuhrable but alsah pretty much entiy'ahly used tah it since that's how it goes.

Brady Gets Suspended

So now Thor n' Loki get back tah Asgard n' they're feelin' all
frazzled aftah that whole fuckin' ohrdeal on the Green Line n'
Odin comes out the front doohr n' is like, "Hey where you guys
been?! You guys ahr missin' out on all the fun. Evuhryone else is
out back right now throwin' shit at Brady[96] since nothin' can evah
huhrt him since he's mihraculous n' the best fuckin' quahtahback'ah all time."

N' so ah'couhrse Thor's like, "Shit! That sounds fuckin' awesome!" N' he runs right out back, n' Loki follows him, tah where
evuhryone else is throwin' shit at Brady.

Now I mean they're throwin' all sohrts'ah shit at Brady. He's
gettin' fuckin' freshly shahpened hockey skates thrown at him,
fuckin' DD cups, fuckin' lobstah traps, hell I think one guy even
threw the city's entiyah fuckin' snowpile from 2015 at the guy,
but nothin' even so much as fuckin' scrapes him since he's just
that good.

Now the reason Brady was gettin' all this shit thrown at him is
that he was havin' all these wicked bad nightmahrs 'bout gettin'
injuh'd on the field n' all which freaked the guy out n' so he went
n' he told Odin n' evuhryone else 'bout it. So at that point, all the
gods, they did the whole shrink thing fahr him fah r'awhile but
then they decided that the best thing tah do in this pahticulah situation would be tah have Frigg go 'round the whole wide wohrld

---

96 As discussed earlier in the footnote 65 on page 65 of *The
Mistreatment of a Deviant's Ballsack*, the ancient tradition of
the fair god, Balder, has been subsumed and hybridized with
the newer tradition of the patriot god, Tom Brady, in *The
Impudent Edda*.

n' have evuhry livin' n' non-livin' thing in existence sweahr tah nevah r'evah r'evah r'evah r'evah huhrt Brady evah.[97] N' Frigg didn't mind doin' this any since Brady's her kid n' all n' she's got natuhral mothahly prahtective instincts, n' so she went 'round n' she got evuhry single animate n' inanimate object in existence tah sweahr tah not evah hahm Brady.[98]

Which means that all the gods basic'ly think that he's complete-ly in-fuckin'-vincible now, which is why they all stahted tossin' empty bee'ah bottles n' shit at the guy since nothin' can huhrt him, right. So like that shahpened hockey skate that Skadi just threw at him? Fuckin' just bounced right off his fuckin' face with-out so much as leavin' a scratch. Same thing with that commutah rail train that Thor chucked at his head...

... I think Frey pry threw a fuckin' baculum at the guy...[99]

------

97 The council of the gods and their resolution for Frigg to ex-tract promises of non-injury from inanimate objects also oc-curs in *The Prose Edda*'s *Gylfaginning*, while *Baldrs Draumar*, an ancient Norse poem not found in the original medieval manuscript of *The Poetic Edda* but usually included with modern translations of it, instead describes Odin going on a journey to Hel where he resurrects a dead seeress who then reveals the dire portent of Brady/Balder's bad dreams.

98 In one of the more bizarre scientific undertakings of the an-cient Norse myths, Frigg conducted a very large-scale alchem-ical experiment on all matter in the known universe in which, under presumably highly stringent laboratory conditions, she manipulated the molecular charges of each and every test sam-ple to enhance their properties of inertness. Rather than trying to create the monetarily valuable element of gold from ordinary ore as was frequently the aim of ancient alchemical scientists, her hypothesis instead sought to determine whether any basic element could be altered to acquire the neutral qualities asso-ciated with the noble gases, the idea being that elements that exhibit such properties of non-reactivity would be least likely to react with and potentially detrimentally alter the chemical composition of Brady/Balder's divine molecular structure.

99 This line demarcates the start of *The Impudent Edda*'s poetic aside known as the *Dikbonatal* ("The Delineation of the

A baculum, well it's like a walrus dick bone. I mean, that's just the type'ah thing Frey'd do yah know? Guy's got a one-track mind; he can't stop thinkin' 'bout dicks. But, yah know, it's not like I'm assumin' poohr Brady liked havin' some fuckin' 3 foot long fossilized walrus dick bone thrown at his head. I mean, even if you're fuckin' invincible, who wants a fuckin' walrus dick bone thrown at his head?

Fuckin' like, in Alaska they polish n' decuhrate these dick bones n' use 'em as tools n' magic wands n' shit, I mean they're supposed tah be highly reveeah'd ah somethin' by the Alaskan abahriginals...

I don't know!

I'm not some sohrt'ah dick bone expuhrt. Go ask a fuckin' bahnie. I bet they fuckin' love dick bones ovah r'at Hahvahd. They're all 'bout showin' throbbin' crimson shafts a whole lottah love ovah there.

They might alsah love dick bones ovah r'at MIT too, who knows? Who the fuck even cahrs?

But yah know what, I'll tell yah who doesn't love dick bones.

Thor.

Thor DOES NOT love dick bones. Unless it's his own, then I believe he makes a very special exception.

I mean, it's just that Thor does not strike me as the type'ah guy who'd be standin' out on Yawkey scalpin' dick bones tah passahs-by as way tah pocket some extra cash. I honestly—I just don't see the guy hoahrdin' up dick bones no mattah how hahd up he might be at any given time, like yah know, when Loki fucks him ovah, which happens basic'ly evuhry othah day!

Dick Bones") in which the anonymous scribe detours from the main narrative of the myth for a tangential discussion about certain gods' attitudes toward walrus bacculi, as well as Thor and Loki's numerous, ill-fated attempts to purchase liquor in New Hampshire. While not crucial to the events described in the current myth, an editorial decision was made to maintain the *Dikbonatal* in this edition of *The Impudent Edda* because of its seamless and artful transition linking the narrative of the target practice involving Brady to the narrative of Loki's subsequent traiterous behavior.

According to The Impudent Edda's *poetic aside known as the* Díkbonatal, *Frey threw a walrus dick bone at Brady. This image depicts a particularly ornate walrus dick bone known as an oosik. An oosik is a dick bone—not necessarily of that of a walrus—that has been polished, carved, or otherwise made decorative by native Alaskan culture. This particular oosik features a polar bear head carved into its one end.*

Yeah, like all the times Thor drives his goats up tah Nashua tah stock up on liquah r'n takes Loki 'long with him, which always fucks evuhrything up, since Loki's a mothahfuckin' shape-shiftin' demon sack'ah shit n' he usually just ends up transfohrmin' himself intah some undah r'age kid with a wicked bad fake ID just tah fuck with poohr Thor when they get there.

I sweahr, this happens ALL THE FUCKIN' TIME.

I mean evuhrytime Thor is like, "YES!!! THIS TIME I'M GONNAH FINALLY FUCKIN' DO IT!" thinkin', yah know, that he's gonnah buy all the hahd liquah r'in the entiyah fuckin' state'ah New Hampshah, Loki just then goes n' transfohrms himself intah some pimple faced teenage kid n' now they won't sell tah Thor no mohr since he's accompanied by a fuckin' minah r'n I don't know why Thor keeps takin' him 'long all the time...

N' don't get me wrong, Thor's a great guy n' all, it's just sometimes he's a bit slow.

But Loki, though, he's always been a prick.

Oh n' fuck, he just only gets wohrse 'cause while the gods ahr all out in the backyahd throwin' shit at Brady n' havin' a good time, Loki's just gettin' kindah pissed since good times make him angry since he's an asshole.

So he goes n' he asks Frigg, "Hey Frigg, what the fuck? Why isn't anything huhrtin' Brady any, isn't there anything that can still huhrt Brady?"[100]

N' Frigg, she just goes ahead n' she tells him! Can yah believe that?!?

She's just like, "Oh, well I only evah r'asked a fully fuckin' inflated football tah promise not tah huhrt him, but I nevah bothah'd tah go n' find a fuckin' deflated one n' then extract the same promise outtah it."[101]

So now Loki goes n' he gets himself a football n' then he stahts deflatin' the thing n' then he sees Hod, who's just sittin' on the bench since he's only a back-up god, basic'ly on the fuckin' fahm team n' no one's really payin' any attention tah him ah any'ah the othah Pahtucket guys so Loki goes up tah him n' he asks him why he's not playin'. N' Hod's just like, "'Cause I'm fuckin' blind as a bat, yah fuckin' mohron."

N' then Loki's like, "Oh shit, man, I'm sahrry. Well, hee'ah, I'll help yah guide yah hand if yah wannah go in fah r'a shift." N' so Hod's like yeah, okay, sure, since he's been missin' out n'

----

100 According *The Prose Edda*'s *Gylfaginning*, Loki breaks his molecular symmetry and alters his mass to rearrange his constituent god particles into the form of an unknown elderly woman so that Frigg does not recognize him when he approaches her and inquires about Brady/Balder's invincibility. The author of *The Impudent Edda* quite openly despises Loki and it is unlikely that it was an unintentional oversight that Loki is not presented with the degree of cleverness or caution that a disguise would have validated in this version of the myth.

101 This particular detail has evolved substantially since the time of the Elder Eddas. While *The Poetic Edda* itself does not explicitly discuss Frigg's role of extracting promises from animate and inanimate objects as *The Prose Edda* does, both of the Elder Eddas concur that the illicit object in question in the older tradition of the mythology was the little plant known as mistletoe and not a partially deflated football.

obviously throwin' shit at Brady is the most fun they've had in Asgard since the time they all stood around n' watched Loki get fucked by a hohrse.

So now Hod steps up tah the plate with Loki who helps him toss this deflated piece'ah shit football at Brady n' next thing yah know Indianapolis is throwin' a fuckin' shit fit n' Brady's gettin' the blame fahr Loki's treachahry n' that fuckin' fi'ah demon Goodell sends him down tah Hel fah r'a fuckin' four game suspension n' there ain't even a valkyrie in sight tah escohrt him since he didn't even fall in a real battle.

So all the rest'ah the gods ahr just stunned speechless 'cept fah r'Odin who's just like, "You gottah be fuckin' kiddin' me," since he hates bullshit n' Goodell's stahtin' tah try n' wield powah like he thinks he's a fuckin' god himself.[102]

---

102 The ancient poem, *Baldrs Draumar*, also reveals that Hod not only kills his brother Brady/Balder, but upon having done so, Odin retaliates by having sex with a giantess named Rind, who one day later gives birth to Odin's newest son, Vali, who grows to full manhood in a single day and immediately murders Hod who, being blind, doesn't even see him coming.

Belichick Rides to Hel

So now Frigg hee'ahs 'bout Goodell's god-like prahclahmation n' she's like, "That mothahfuckin' piece'ah shit!" So she goes n' she gets up off her ass n' walks ovah tah the lockah room where evuhryone else is standin' 'round stahrin' at the tv screen watchin' NESN's covah r'age'ah the fuckin' suspension like it's a goddamned muhrdah scene out in Mattapan. So now she sees evuhryone's just mopin' 'round not knowin' what the fuck tah do n' so she decides right then n' there that she bettah take control'ah the whole situation befohr it gets any mohr pathetic n' so she looks 'em all in the eyes n' says, "Alright, so which one'ah yah fuckin' dipshits is gonnah ride down tah Hel tah try n' appeal fahr me on Brady's behalf?"

N' so that's when Belichick the Bold,[103] who's anothah one'ah Odin's many sons, tells Frigg yeah sure he'll drive down tah Hel since Brady's his stah quahtahback, n' so tah help him out a little on his way, Odin gives him the keys tah his eight-legged mustang n' so ah couhrse Belichick thinks this is wicked pissah r'n' so he jumps behind the wheel n' he fi'ahs up that beast n' befohr yah even know it he's peelin' outtah the pahkin' lot ontah Route 1 n' headin' fahr the rainbow bridge like he thinks he's the second comin'ah Mario Andretti ah some shit.

Now all the othah gods who ahr lingah'in' back in the lockah room decide that maybe they ought tah go outside n' get some fresh aihr ah somethin' n' maybe even fi'ah r'up the grills n', yah know, get some fuckin' tail gatin' action goin' so as tah try n' get their mind's off'ah Brady's predicahment. So they're all out there now in

---

103 In *The Impudent Edda*, Belichick the Bold has taken on
 the role traditionally held by Hermod in *The Prose Edda*'s
 Gylfaginning.

the pahkin' lot grillin' n' drinkin' n' things ahr still kindah sombah but at least they're not just standin' 'round mopin' like they were befohr when things staht tah get really fuckin' weihrd.

So at this point some damned giantess ridin' a fuckin' wolf gets lost on her way tah Rhode Island n' decides tah pull up next tah where the gods ahr grillin' out in the pahkin' lot tah ask fahr dihrections. Well, four'ah Odin's buhzehrkahs just flip the fuck out 'cause no way some fuckin' giantess's got the right tah crash their fuckin' funahral tail-gatin' pahty n' so they go buhzehrk n' fuckin' kill that bitch right there on the spot, which evuhyrone else thought was wicked good en-tahtainment 'cept fahr Gisele[104] who just can't handle this degree'ah senseless violence on top'ah all the othah bullshit that's happened tah her husband lately n' so she ends up havin' a bit of a nehrvous break-down but then Sif stahts talkin' tah her 'bout the beaches in Brazil n' this helps get her mind off'ah things at least fahr'a bit.

N' all while this is happenin', Ole One-Eye's just mindin' the grill n' flippin' the buhrgahs but one'ah his special rings somehow ends up slippin' off'ah his fingah by accident n' intah the grill n' he loses the thing in the flames, which sucks.[105] But the best paht'ah the whole pahty had tah be when some dumb dwahrf popped up from outtah nowhere n' Thor got all pissed 'bout n' kicked the little bastahd straight intah the fuckin' flames![106] HA![107]

---

104 *The Impudent Edda* displays a late case of German-Brazil-ian influence here in its assertion that Brady/Balder's wife is named Gisele rather than the more traditional Nanna as is the case in the Elder Eddas and other medieval source material.

105 While unnamed, the magic ring in question is almost cer-tainly Draupnir, which was forged by the dwarf gang known as the Hel's Valkyries, as described on page 21 of *Wicked Good Dwarf Treasure*.

106 It is unclear how exactly a dwarf, upon having been kicked by the strongest of the gods, would nonetheless be small enough to fall through one of the gaps in the cooking grate of the grill being manned by Odin. The Norse myths have historically always been full of logical incongruencies and inconsistences, and this instance is no exception.

107 *The Impudent Edda* deviates substantially from *The Prose*

But anyway, while all this is goin' on, Belichick the Bold's made his way down tah Hel n' so now he's pahkin' Odin's eight-legged mustang n' feedin' the fuckin' meetah r'n he heads intah the Couhrt'ah Appeals n' comes 'cross this cranky receptionist bitch n' she looks at him n' she's like, "Hey, what the fuck ahr yah doin' hee'ah? Yah don't look like a lawyah tah me."

N' ah'couhrse Belichik's no fuckin' lawyah so he's like, "What the fuck?!? I'm just lookin' fahr my stah quahtahback, yah seen—"

But that rude bitch just cuts him off n' tells him where he needs tah go n' then goes back tah readin' 'bout the undahwohrld's thihrty-nine newest ways tah reach ohrgasm as fast as possible ah whatevah r'in her Cosmo magazine. So Belichik gets on the fuckin' elevatah r'n goes down tah the basement like he was in-

---

Edda in its relating of the activities immediately following the suspension/death of Brady/Balder, which traditionally has been one of the most somber yet cinematographic in all of Norse mythology. As related in the *Gylfaginning*, the gods did not start tail-gating at Gillete Stadium, but rather prepared a ship-borne funeral pyre for the fallen hero. Brady/Balder's boat, however, was of such magnificence and weight that the gods could not tow it across land (from where it was kept in the off-season) to the water themselves and so instead they enlisted the help of the wolf-riding giantess, Hyrrokkin, who obliges and, notably, does not get murdered by the berserkers, though her wolf does. At this point, Brady/Balder's corpse is carried and placed on the boat while Gisele/Nanna dies from grief and is subsequently laid beside him. The pyre is then lit, and as Thor steps forward to consecrate it with his mighty hammer, a dwarf runs in front of him, which he then kicks into the flames. After Thor's holy consecration of the pyre/ritualistic act of dwarf murder, Odin intentionally places his magic ring, Draupnir, in the flames and Brady/Balder's horse is slaughtered and also placed on the pyre. Finally, with gods, elves, dwarves, valkyries, and even some giants in full attendance, Brady/Balder's boat is pushed out to sea in truly epic Viking fashion, burning brightly against the darkening sky as the final doom of the gods looms ever closer.

The Tjäng-videsten from Alskog, Sweden illustrates several motifs from Viking Age era Scandinavian life, most notably the eight-legged wonder-horse known as Sleipnir that Odin allows Belichick to borrow for his ride down to Hel.

structed tah do n' then finally finds the doohr tah Hel's office n' he opens it n' goes right on in since, he's like, yah know, he's the head coach.

N' sure 'nough he sees Hel sittin' there in that dingy basement office suhrrounded by hundreds n' hundreds'ah empty styrafoam DD cups while Brady's just sittin' there in a chair off tah the side like a little kid in time out next tah poohr fuckin' Chahlie who nevah paid his exit faihre n' has been stuck in this shithole since the fuckin' '60s. So Belichik gives Brady a nod n' goes straight up tah Hel n' he inqui'ahs 'bout Brady's fuckin' fate n' Hel's just like, "Eh, he's stuck down hee'ah till someone pays the prahpah fuckin' exit faihre."

N' so Belichik tries tah give her a nickel since he's heahrd this song befohr but now the goddamned transit authahrity's gone n' jacked up the prices all ovah 'gain n' so now it's gonnah cost the gods a lot mohr 'en just a fuckin' five-cent piece just tah set Brady free n' this one's not gonnah be the sohrt'ah ticket yah can just download on yah fuckin' iphone n' then fahget 'bout it.[108]

But if those gods don't figyah out how tah pay this fuckin' tax pretty soon then poohr Brady's gonnah end up sittin' out mohr 'en just the staht'ah the season but on the upside he's got poohr fuckin' Chahlie there tah keep him company, so at least he's not all alone.

---

108 As with the events surrounding Brady/Balder's tail-gate party/funeral, the scene involving Belichick/Hermod's ride to Hel and encounter with the demon woman of the same name deviates drastically from the earlier rendition provided by *The Prose Edda*. The version preserved in the *Gylfaginning* portrays Belichick/Hermod as riding Odin's eight-legged steed, Sleipnir, for nine whole days en route to Hel before he reaches the Gjoll Bridge which separates the land of the living from the land of the dead. There, he encounters the maiden, Modgud, who inquires about his ancestry—since that was always of utmost importance in medieval times— and also confirms that Brady/Balder rode over the same bridge sometime earlier. Belichick/Hermod crosses the bridge and continues on the road to Hel till he reaches the Gates of Hel, leaps over them upon Sleipnir and enters Hel's hall where he sees his brother, Brady/Balder, sitting in the seat of honor, but with no sign of Charlie anywhere. After spending the night, he asks Hel if she would be willing to release his brother and she responds that she would, but only if every living and non-living thing in the known universe will weep on Brady/Balder's behalf. Belichick/Hermod pre- pares to return to Asgard, but before he departs Brady/Bald- er gives him the ring, Draupnir, to return to their father, Odin, and Gisele/Nanna (who is dead in *The Prose Edda*'s version of the myth at this point) hands him a robe to give to Frigg, and a gold ring to give to Fulla, the infrequently mentioned goddess whose primary responsibility is to keep Frigg's insanely massive assortment of shoes in order and under control.

Loki Swims with the Fishes

So now poohr fuckin' Brady's trapped in a shitty subway station 'neath the Second Distric Couhrt'ah Appeals in FUCKIN' NEW YOHRK with that bitch Hel and that goofy bastahd Chahlie while Belichick's racin' back tah Frigg n' Odin n' all the othahs so's that he can tell'em that they gottah convince evuhry damn thing in the whole wide wohrld tah cry on Brady's behalf in orhdah tah lift the suspension on their stah quahrtahback. N' if at fihrst they don't succeed, well then the entiyah fuckin' univehrse is gonnah get scohrched like a fuckin' nucleah holocaust since that's the type'ah hahrdco'ah shit that these Viking guys believed back in those days.

But the gods though, they send out these messengahs tah all ovah the fuckin' place, n' they're gettin' evuhryone n' evuhrything tah cry fahr Brady 'cept fahr this one old giantess[109] who's hidin' in a crevice in a granite quahrry up in Quebec all alone by herself n' she's pissed at the wohrld n' so she refuses tah weep fahr him since she's a bitch n' yah know what that means...

...EVERYTHING IS FUCKED!!!
EVERYTHING!!![110]

There is no come-back. This is not like game 7 'gainst Tahronto back in '13 where mihracles really do happen late in the 3rd. I'm

---

109 *The Prose Edda's Gylfaginning* reveals that this giantess' name is especially feminine-sounding: Thokk.

110 In the original recording of *The Impudent Edda*, the author's already questionable sobriety undergoes a marked decrease beginning with this myth, from whence it only continues to deteriorate further up until the final seconds of the final myth.

tellin' yah, this is mohr like regulah season n' not makin' the play-offs at all. But the gods though, they all think that this giantess was actually Loki in disguise which is on accoun'ah him bein' the biggest shit-stick on the planet n' ah'couhrse now he knows that the gods ahr gonnah be on his ass like white on rice n' so he takes off n' he goes n' he finds a hidin' place up somewhere deep in the White Mountains. N' so as tah try n' blend in bettah with his local suhrroundings, he holes himself up there in some cabin somewhere n' then—get this—he prahceeds tah tuhrn himself in-tah a fuckin' fish! Can yah believe that? N' then, I guess he just goes swimmin' in the rivah[111] r'out back 'cause, well, he's a fish now... fuck, man...I haven't been fishin' in so long...

But fuck Loki though, fuck him. Fuck him, I sweaahhhrrrr... okay, n' so sometimes he gets kindah boah'd with bein' a fuckin' fish 'cause, yah know, who wants tah be a fuckin' fish, right? I mean, at this point he pry wished he'd stolen Frigg's falcon outfit 'gain,[112] but he didn't think'ah that in his rush tah get outtah Asgard. Anyway, bein' a fish is fuckin' stupid n' so ah'couhrse sometimes even Loki's gottah take a break from bein' a fish n' all n' so he goes n' he uhh, well, he basic'ly just sits by his fi'ah place where he fantasizes 'bout his own death since he's a sick fuckin' bastahd n' fahr some reason the fuckin' idiot goes n' he makes a fuckin' fishin' net.

That's right, a fuckin' fishin net.

So now what we got is Loki just sittin' there lookin' at this net like it's a fuckin' noose since fahr'a fish it pretty much fuckin' is, which is when the rest'ah the gods all entah r'intah his house! So he throws the fuckin' thing intah the fi'ah r'n runs out back where he prahceeds to jump back intah the rivah r'in fish fohrm 'gain.

---

111 According to the *Gylfaginning* in *The Prose Edda*, Loki spends the majority of his time as a fish swimming in the waterfall or rapids (it is unclear which) known as Franang's Falls. It is plausible that this could be in New Hampshire, as stated here.

112 Loki's obsession with avian transmogrifiers apparently continues right up until the final moments of his exile. For more on his theft of Frigg's transmogrifier, see page 97 of *Thor Wades Through the Menstrual Fluid Fjord*.

*A tranquil northern New England river rapids scene, which
is also where it has been prophesied that Loki will taunt
Thor with his superior aquatic swimming abilities as a fish.*

But the gods, yah know, they weren't bohrn yestahday n' so
they see the ashes'ah that net n' they figyah it out. They're like,
"OH FUCK, LOOK AT THAT. IT'S A FUCKIN' FISHIN' NET.
LOKI MUST BE SWIMMIN' LIKE A FISH IN THE RIVAH
RIGHT NOW. LET'S GO KILL THAT STUPID SON OF A
BITCH."[113]

---

113 According to the *Gylfaginning*, the god that first notices the
   ashes of the net and its potential significance is Kvasir, who
   in *The Impudent Edda*'s version of the mythology is first
   created from spittle on page 17 in *How Not to Get Away with
   Witch Murder* and subsequently murdered by a couple of
   dwarf gang members on page 36 in *Blood Spit Honey Death*.
   Curiously enough, *The Prose Edda* also states that Kvasir is
   murdered by dwarves, and it goes completely unexplained
   as to how he could still be alive much later in order to help

N' so they go on out back down tah the rivah r'n the gods, they're lovin' that clean n' clee'ah cool mountain watah 'cause it ain't like that muhrky shit watah like we got 'round hee'ah. N' alsah, it means that the gods can actually SEE all those fuckin' fish THROUGH THE WATAH with their OWN EYES.

N' so now they're standin' there 'round the fuckin' rivah stahrin' at the fuckin' watah, tryin' tah spot Loki n' there's a fuckin' ton a fish in the watah! N' I guess it's gottah be that clean cool mountain aihr that's good fahr the fish's lungs ah whatevah that does it but yah know…it means they gottah play a little game'ah ripahrian Where's Waldo fahr now since the rivah's so fuckin' full'ah fishes.

N' so as I've been tellin' yah all 'long, Thor is not exactly what one would call a patient individual. So like maybe all the othah gods ahr just standin' there keepin' their cool, countin' the fish, but not Thor. Thor's a fuckin' fightah r'n so he's gettin' himself all wohrked up intah one'ah his killin' moods n' the stohrm clouds ahr stahtin' tah gathah r'ovahhead n' so if they don't spot Loki pretty soon so that he can go n' open up a full-on can'ah angry thundah god whoop ass on Loki then they bettah pray tah… well I guess they bettah pray tah 'emselves. But regahdless, they bettah pray that there's at least a shit-ton'ah bee'ah back in the fuckin' fridge 'cause the only thing that stands a chance'ah appeasin' Thor right now othah 'en killin' some fuckin' fish is gettin' drunk. The guy's a fuckin' lush.

---

capture Loki. This is most likely an oversight/editing error on Snorri Sturlason's part, but since he was murdered 800 years ago this could not be confirmed at the time of the printing of this edition of *The Impudent Edda*.

Snake Poison Torture Time

So now the gods ahr all just standin' 'round by the fuckin' rivah watchin' Loki swim 'round like a fuckin' fish. Which he is, I guess, since he transfohrmed his dumb ass intah one n' so now he's doin' fuckin' swan dives n' back flips n' shit just tah egg 'em all on till Thor finally fuckin' loses it n' just dives in head fihrst aftah the slippahry bastahd!

N' he's lucky he missed the fuckin' rocks too! Not that it did him any good in the long run though since he's already got a fuckin' whetsone lodged in his skull from some othah brawl he got intah a while back with some giant asshole[114] but now, he basic'ly snatches that piece'ah shit Loki right outtah thin aihr while he's doin' some flippity-flop like some sohrt'ah acrobatic at the summah r'Olympics ah somethin' n' I tell yah, he just fuckin' crushes that mothahfuckahs tail right then n' there with his bare

---

114 While the story of the whetsone lodged in Thor's head only receives passing mention in *The Impudent Edda*, it is described in colorful detail in *The Prose Edda*'s *Skáldskapar-mál*, in which Thor engages in a one-on-one personal duel with the evil giant Hrungnir. During the climax of this duel, Thor hurled his hammer at Hrungnir, who himself threw his own weapon of choice, a whetstone (an odd choice, but Hrungnir was admittedly a nonconformist), at Thor. The hammer and whetstone collided in mid-air, and while the hammer went on to strike and kill Hrungnir where he stood, the whetstone broke into two pieces, one of which struck Thor in the head, where it has been lodged ever since (the advanced surgical techniques necessary to remove it had not yet been developed at the time of this event).

hands, n' now this is the reason why all the Nahwegians think that salmon's got nahrrow tails...[115]

...but yeah, so now we got Thor who's thinkin' it'd be a wicked good idea tah fuckin' flay Loki alive right there on the fuckin' spot since he loves violence n' the immediate gratification that goes 'long with killin' but NNNOOOOOOOO. All the othah gods ahr like, "Uh, we can't do that Thor, we need tah fuckin' tohrt'ah his ass instead." N' FAH THOR THIS FUCKIN' SUCKS!!! I mean fahr him this is like... uh, well, it's like uh... uh... well it's like losin' the signal on yah cell phone, I guess. N' yah know, not bein' able tah update yah status fahr the rest'ah the day since it's, yah know, it's all 'bout the instant gratification n' the petty distraction that makes yah feel like you're less alone in life. But as a way tah try n' appease Thor since he's got a nasty fuckin' tempah, the rest'ah the gods give him a couple'ah kegs'ah stout since it's Saint Patty's Day[116] n' all n' he loves gettin' shitfaced as much as evuhry othah red-haihred bastahd in this fuckin' town.

So now the gods, they all go n' they lock Loki up in a fuckin' cave somewhere out in the middle'ah fuckin' I don't even know where n' it doesn't even mattah 'cept fahr the fact that Thor's not there since he's already finished off his kegs'ah Guinness n' has moved ontah binge-drinkin' green-coluh'd Budweisahs with the guys from the BC hockey team who ahr still celebratin' their victahry ovah BU at all the touristy spots 'round Faneuil Hall. N' so he's off actin' like a fuckin' hooligan ah whatevah with the cool

---

115 *The Prose Edda*'s *Gylfaginning* version of this myth relates a much more elaborate and highly orchestrated effort to capture Loki that involved all of the gods (not just Thor) and a special net that they had expressly made just for this purpose. Loki attempts to jump over the net and is captured by Thor mid-air, somewhat similar to his capture as portrayed in *The Impudent Edda*'s rendition.

116 The fact that Loki's capture occurred on March 17th is a very new and important detail never before revealed in any of the earlier Eddic sources. Saint Patrick's role in *The Impudent Edda* likewise is a previously unbeknownst detail that sheds new light on the origins of the snake that Skadi keeps in her possession as described on the next page

kids[117] n'... uh... well, the rest'ah the gods kidnap Loki's nahmal sons[118] n' they fuckin' transfohrm one'ah 'em intah a fuckin' wolf n' yah know what this wolf does? He fuckin' muhrdahs Loki's othah nahmal son! He fuckin' MUHRDAHS him!

I don't know why. 'Cause it's what wolves who used tah be people ahr supposed tah do?

Well, it's what the gods wanted... I mean, obviously this was intentional on their paht 'cause next thing yah know they take that poohr kids' entrails n' they fuckin' tie Loki up with 'em n'... yeah these are the good guy gods we're talkin' 'bout!

... I mean yeah, I know Loki's a real piece'ah shit, but goddamn.

So next, Skadi just so happens tah have this poisonous snake with her that she's cahrried 'round allovah the place evah since Patty boy chased the fuckin' thing outtah Ireland n'... aahhhh, I'm not sure when that was, but I think it was a while back. It's a whole diffuhrent stahry altagethah.

Anyway, I guess yah just nevah know when yah might need tah have a poisonous snake on hand tah tohrtah someone with n' in this case it tuhrned out tah come in pretty handy. I mean, it's fuckin' practical! If yah lookin' tah tohrtah a demonic Nahrse god

---

117 Beginning here, *The Impudent Edda* deviates from all other primary sources regarding Thor's behavior and whereabouts following Loki's capture. The Elder Eddas generally concur that Thor continued to keep the company of his fellow Aesir, rather than going off solo on an all-night bender in downtown Boston in the final days leading up to the collective doom that finally destroys them all.

118 *The Prose Edda*'s *Gylfaginning* reveals that Loki's sons are named Vali and Nari/Narfi (Snorri appears to have been confused about the exact spelling of the second son) while the *Lokasenna* in *The Poetic Edda* reveals that the names are Nari (rather than Vali) and Narfi; the two Elder Eddas do not agree on this particular matter nor on the specific events. The *Lokasenna*'s version does not involve one brother-turned-wolf ripping the other brother to shreds. The *Lokasenna* does, however, concur that one was turned into a wolf while the other was gutted (but without any specific details as to how).

The New England Holocaust Memorial in downtown Boston. It has been foretold that Thor will vomit all over himself and pass out drunk beneath its glass towers during the events immediately preceding Ragnarök.

anyway that is. But yeah, so Skadi she goes n' she like, she somehow like drapes the fuckin' thing ovah r'a rock right there above Loki's head n' I guess it just stays there… like it doesn't even try tah slithah r'away ah r'anything…

I don't know, maybe Patty boy hit it too hahd on the head with his fuckin' shillelagh ah somethin', I don't know.

But now it's got a fuckin' mental defect ah somethin'. I mean the dumb thing just lays there without evah r'even movin' n' basic'ly it just sits there n' fuckin' drools buhrnin' hot venom down all ovah Loki's fuckin' face fahr the rest'ah etuhrnity, 'cept fahr, yah know, when the entiyah fuckin' wohrld ends in a huge fuckin' fi'ahball'ah death n' destruction at the end'ah time.

But alsah his wife, Sigyn, helps him out most'ah the time by catchin' the poison drool in a bowl which is pretty nice'ah her since she doesn't have tah be there n' she's missin' the pahrade down Broadway on accoun'ah this shit.[119]

But poohr fuckin' Thor, man! That guy! What a fuckin' guy. So he's alsah droolin' right now but that's only on accoun'ah the fact that he's passed out face down on one the steam vents ovah r'at the Holocaust Memahrial aftah he got himself kicked outtah the Oystah House fahr pukin' all ovah JFK's honah'ahry table... n' yeah, now the guy's bein' a fuckin' vagrant like Odin. Jesus Christ. At least when Loki was 'round he didn't drink himself tah fuckin' oblivion, but at the same time, he really fuckin' knows how tah get intah the spirit'ah the holiday. I think he even wore a green cape this time.

119 *The Impudent Edda* bypasses a powerful detail here that is fortunately not lost in either of the Elder Eddas: that whenever Sigyn leaves Loki's side to empty the bowl of poisonous venom, the venom that drips down upon his face in the interim results in extreme pain and his violent thrashing, which is the source of all earthquakes in Middle-Earth. As with Old Norse astrophysics, the science behind Old Norse geotectonics deviates dramatically from our current understandings of natural phenomena.

Thor Breaks and Enters into a Dunkin' Donuts

So like I'as telling yah, Thor's been passed out, yah know, just sleepin' it off undah some wicked deep pile'ah snow on the side'ah the road ovah by Haymahket since fuckin' Saint Patty's Day but then he finally wakes the fuck up 'cause now his stomach's stahtin' tah growl n' he needs tah eat some food fah r'is fuckin' hangovah. So he digs himself outtah his snow mound n' he goes n' he stumbles on ovah tah the neeh'ast street cohrnah tah get his food but then it tuhrns out that the DD is FUCKIN' CLOSED SINCE THE ENTIYAH FUCKIN' CITY'S SHUT-DOWN LIKE THE WINTAH'AH 2015 NEVAH R'EVEN FUCKIN' ENDED!

Now natruhly this is some real heahrt-breakin' news fahr poohr Thor since he's fuckin' stahvin' but just tah be clee'ah, he doesn't give a rat's ass 'bout the snow. This is fuckin' Thor we're talkin' 'bout hee'ah! FUCKIN' THOR!!! HE FUCKIN' THRIVES ON THIS SHIT. ICE, SNOW, SLUSH, ROAD SALT, MUD SEASON, FUCKIN' WHATEVAH…I MEAN HE'S FUCKIN' FROM THE LAND OF THE ICE N' SNOW…N' HIS HAM-MAH WILL DRIVE OUR SHIPS TO NEW LANDS!!!

TO FIGHT THE HORDE, SINGIN' N' CRYIN', VALLL-HALLLLAAAAAAA I AM COMING!!!![120]

---

120 While such instances occur with much less frequency in *The Impudent Edda* in comparison to other primary sources, the recitation of an earlier, related work (usually in poetic format) known to the author is a common convention in Eddic literature. In this case, while it goes unstated in specific terms by the author himself, he is drawing on verses attributed to the great 20th century English skald, Robert

Sometimes yah just gottah get the led out, yah know?

But in tehrms'ah tempahs, fuckin' no one tops Thor. Fuckin' no one. He's got an even shohrtah fuse 'en Terry O'Reilly but he doesn't have tah go n' climb on ovah the boahrds just tah staht a fuckin' fight with the fans 'cause he's gottah couple'ah demented goats that'll do all the climbin' fahr him. N' he can fuckin' whip out Mjölnir whenevah the fuck he feels like!

NO!!!

Mjölnir is not his dick. It's his hammah.

HIS HAMMAH IS NAMED MJÖLNIR. WITH A FUCKIN' R AT THE END.

I don't know what his dick is named. Maybe Thor Jr.? Ah how 'bout Lil' Thundahstick? Yah know, since he's the thundah god n' all...

...well I don't know but could be, bein' as he's a fuckin' gingah n' all... yeah, Hollywood got that one WAY FUCKIN' OFF. Fuckin' mohrons.

Well, yeah so he's fuckin' stahvin' since he ain't eaten since he blacked out back in Mahch n' so now he whips out his Mjölnir so as tah break intah the fuckin' DD.

Because he wants to eat all the breakfast sandwiches! The guy's fuckin' stahved! I TOLD YOU THIS ALREADY. He ain't eaten since Mahch n' he doesn't give a flyin' fuck 'bout ahrganic ah locally grown whatevah. He just wants a GODDAMNED BREAKFAST SANDWICH IS ALL. N' alsah maybe a donut ah two.

Yeah, so he uses his magic hammah—NOT HIS DICK—tah break n' entah r'intah the DD like a fuckin' delinquint but then he realizes that he doesn't know how tah opahrate the special oven n' all the sandwiches are frozen fuckin' solid n' so he sits his ass down n' he stahts cryin' n' eventually he falls tah sleep n' so now he's layin' there on the floh'ah, snoozin' like some homeless bastahd when his ahchnemesis the Middle-Earth Demon Sehrpent Snake ah whatevah the fuck that thing is, suddenly wakes up n' rises up from OUTTAH THE OCEAN. N' next thing yah know this goddamned dejehnahrut reptile's slithah

---

Plant, which is indirectly acknowledged by the author in the line that follows in the main body of the text.

The Dunkin' Donuts on North Street in Boston facing the historic Faneuil Hall marketplace. It is here that Thor will commit petty larceny after waking up on the street with a massive hangover.

r'in his way on up tah sho'ah r'ovah r'at Revee'ah Beach so he can fill up on some roast beef sandwiches befohr stahtin' on his killin' spree downtown.

Now this would not'ah happened had Thor gotten the fuckin' nourishment he needed! THOR FUCKIN' RUNKIN ON DUNKIN!!! Ah somethin' like that...I don't know, but sounds good, right? Shit, I bet that slogan'd sure as hell sell some extra Big N' Toasties if yah ask me.

But yeah, so the poohr fuckin' guy's passed out from malnourishment and so now there's no one tah stop the fuckin' snake who's at this point bahrrelin' down 1A like he's runnin' late fah r'a fuckin' flight. Now at the EXACT same time as this, Loki's othah jehrk-off son, the Fenriswolf, busts outtah his ribbon-chains from up off the coast'ah Maine somewhere n' so now that guy's drivin' down 95 like a fuckin' whackjob in zero visibility white-out conditions 'cause the snow's comin' down like a fuckin' bitch.[121] N' not that it really mattahs anyways since no one can see 'em anymohr anyway due tah the fuckin' blizzahd conditions out there but anothah couple'ah wolves just jumped up from outtah fuckin' nowhere n' swallah'd the sun n' the moon, so now the sky's just all totally gone tah shit. N' tah really fuckin' top it all off, down ovah r'at South Station the Amtrak crashes intah the commutah rail n' lets loose a shitton'ah asshole New Yohrkahs who ahr now stahtin' tah swahrm the city like a fuckin' plague.[122]

---

121 While most of this myth does not have a direct correlation in either of the Elder Eddas, at this point in his telling it is presumed that the author is introducing the well-known Fimbulwinter, which is attested to in both of the earlier works. The Fimbulwinter constitutes six extreme winters in uninterrupted succession that precede Ragnarök. During the Fimbulwinter, brother will kill brother and father will kill son. The wolf, Skoll, will swallow the sun and the wolf, Månegarm, will swallow the moon, spattering blood across the sky and obscuring the stars which will then disappear from view. In the words of *The Poetic Edda*'s *Völuspá*, it is an axe-age, blade-age, wind-age, and wolf-age and none shall be spared. The earth will tremble, trees will whither, and mountains will fall as the impending doom of the gods now very rapidly approaches.

122 With this sequence of events, Ragnarök has officially begun. While *The Impudent Edda* generally follows the older tradition set forth in the Elder Eddas regarding the Fenriswolf's escape from his bonds and the Middle-Earth serpent's emergence from the sea, it deviates drastically in its depiction of the train full of invasive New Yorkers. The Elder Eddas instead relate that the sons of Muspellsheim, evil fire giants, will split asunder the sky as they descend upon the field of battle to bring death and destruction to all.

Everyone and Everything Dies

So now as if havin' all these goddamned Yankees fans prowlin' 'round town's not bad 'nough, just tah make mattahs even wohrse some shitty ass boat made outtah a bunch'ah decayed toenails docks ovah next tah the aquahrium n' lets loose the entiyah squad'ah those jehrk-off Habs[123] while at the same time that fuckin' fi'ah demon Roger Goodell[124] jumps up from outtah the sewahs covah'd in piss n' shit n' stahts mahchin' down Chahrles Street flingin' flamin' feces like a dehranged monkey since he's such a sick n' twisted fuck. N' so ah course Loki sees this shit n' he's like, "If that fuckin' douchebag can manipulate the system n' get away with it then so can I since I'm an actual evil fuckin' god," n' so then he goes n' he breaks his magical chains n' escapes from that dahk cave up there somewheres in New Hampshah n' ends up hitchhikin' his ass back all the way intah town.

So now yah got this hahrible situation where all these fuckin' freaks ahr stahtin' tah convehrge on the Common n' Heimdall who's supposed tah be on the lookout fahr this type'ah shit's too busy buhryin' his sahrrows intah pint aftah fuckin' pint'ah Hahpoon IPA ovah r'at at his favuhrite Irish pub on Beacon Street instead'ah standin' out in front'ah the Freedom Trail visitah cen-

---

123 The Elder Eddas have identified this ship made of dead men's nails as Naglfar, and that it is crewed by evil frost giants, rather than the entire roster of the Montreal Canadians, longtime rivals of the Boston Bruins.

124 While universally vilified for good reason by the New England populace, Roger Goodell's role in the twilight of the gods has traditionally been held in all other primary sources by the fire giant named Surt.

*Several manholes at an intersection on Charles Street in the
Beacon Hill neighborhood. It is from one of these that the evil
fire giant known as Goodell will emerge from the sewers, fling-
ing shit, and usher in the beginning of the twilight of the gods.*

tah in his colonial atti'yah like he oughtah been, finally sees that
goddamned sehrpent slithah right on past the window outside n'
he just 'bout shits a brick but then he runs n' he gets his special
hohrn[125] n' he stahts blowin' on it like the fuckin' British ahr
comin' so as tah wake Odin the fuck up since that guy's been
sleepin' it off ovah r'on the stoop in front'ah the Asgard on Mass
Ave aftah he got shit-faced there the night befohr when the nice
young gihrl he was hittin' on shot his wrinkly old ass down.

---

125 *The Prose Edda*'s *Gylfaginning* reveals that this horn is called
Gjallarhorn. The imagery of Heimdall's blowing of the Gjallarhorn is recreated in altered but spectacular detail in the
final battle of *The Two Towers* film, when Gimli the dwarf
blows into the horn at Helm's Deep as the tide of the battle
for Rohan's existence turns.

So now evuhryone's woken up n's gettin' ready, n' all the gods ahr gearin' up in their best suits'ah ahmah r'n Bobby Orr n' Big Papi n' Gronk n' all the rest'ah Odin's guys ahr lacin' up in the lockah room n' pretty soon they're all stahtin' tah stohrm outtah the Meadhall's five hundred n' fohrty doohrs[126] straight on tahwahrds the rivah r'n they're all crossin' the salt n' peppah bridge now n' so they meet up with Odin n' Heimall n' all the othah gods outside'ah MGH n' tahgethah they all staht walkin' tahwahrds the Common n' Odin's in the lead right next tah Ray Bourque who's still cahrryin' the Cup but Odin, he thought he'd mix it up a bit fahr the occasion so instead'ah the usual wizahd robe he's weahrin' a Pats jehrsey with his Gandalf hat in honah'ah Brady who's still havin' tah sit this one out since he's been fohrced tah chill out down in Hel evah since he got fucked ovah fahr bein' the best in the entiyah league by that same fuckin' fi'ah demon who's busy flingin' shit all ovah Beacon Hill right now.

N' fuckin', poohr Brady man! He's sittin' this whole fuckin' battle out due tah his suspension by the shit-flingin' fi'ah demon, but on the upside he suhrvives even aftah Goodell sets himself on fi'ah n' accidentally buhrns down the entiyah fuckin' univehrse n' then ah'couhrse he goes on tah win anothah Supahbowl aftahwahds! IN FUCKIN' OVAHTIME!!![127]

---

126 The meadhall in question is known as Valhalla, the hall of the slain, in the Elder Eddas and the heroes who rush out of its five hundred and forty doors (the specific quantity is affirmed by the *Grímnismál* in *The Poetic Edda*) are known as the Einherjar, Odin's own personal troop of undead warriors whose souls have been plucked up by the valkyries upon their death in battle on the human plane of existence in Middle-Earth.

127 This statement is another example of the fluidity of the space-time continuum as conceptualized in the ancient Norse manner of thinking. While *The Impudent Edda*'s recording has been accurately and confidently dated to June 12, 2019, the anonymous poet nonetheless speaks here of grand events that are known to have happened on February 5, 2017 as though they are still yet to happen. It should also be reiterated that the historical record indicates that the poet of *The Impudent Edda* is very inebriated at this stage in his performance.

Norse motif on the Longfellow Bridge, also known as the Salt and Pepper Bridge. The bridge crosses the Charles River from Cambridge to Boston and will provide an appropriate backdrop for the gods when they march towards their impending doom. A Red Line train full of oblivious commuters and students will presumably rumble by at precisely the same moment.

I'm not sure what happens tah Gisele…
…Goodell's a fuckin' prick…
What?
Don't even fuckin' staht with me on this. I sweahr tah fuckin' God…
I PUT A HOLE IN THE WALL OVAH R'AT THE RINK IN MALDEN!!!
Now that was a fuckin' battle'ah epic prahpohrtions…
My Malden stahry's fuckin' poignant n' epic as fuck…
… yeah, it's a good stahry, sometimes it's even kindah fuckin' poetic, like if Robert Frost were tah have gotten ejected fahr fightin' in a men's D league hockey game n' stahted ohratin' Beow-

ulf back in the lockah room just to let off some steam but then fuckin' punched the wall anyways…

… well, 'cause sometimes punchin' the wall is just fuckin' theauhrapeutic! I bet Robert Frost punched a shit-ton'ah walls back in his day. N' then I bet he went n' he mended 'em like a fuckin' lunatic ah some shit, I don't know…

… but yeah, so Odin—who really does love the Pats by the way—so now he's makin' his way through Beacon Hill n' he's really fuckin' hopin' that Shelley Long's finished up her shift n' got out safe n' sound befohr that fuckin' NFL commissionah showed up n' stahted smeah r'in' the bah r'in human manoo'ah r'n it's right 'bout now that Thor finally wakes the fuck up from where he's been sleepin' it off ovah r'at the DD. So he gets his ass up n' he gohrges himself on some frozen hash browns since at this point he's just like who the fuck even cares if they're cold ah not, the wohrld's 'bout tah fuckin' end n' he needs some goddamned nourishment if he's gonnah go n' ahrm wrestle that piece-ah-shit Middle-Earth Sehrpent Snake fah r'once n' fah r'all n' so now he's all cahb-loaded up n' caffeinated outtah his fuckin' mind n' so he rushes out ovah tah where the gods n' their wahrriahs ahr prepahrin' tah take the field n' he joins up with his old man on the stahtin' line n' tahgethah they walk out ontah the couhrt at the Public Gahden with Larry Bird, Bill Russell, n' John Havlicek since it's time tah beat the fuckin' shit outtah LA, n' so the rest'ah the gods, they n' their buddies, they all take the field on the Common n' then they all just staht fuckin' fightin' their rivals, yah know? So like Heimdall n' Loki, those two guys basic'ly just kill each othah right on the fuckin' spot, right? N' ovah r'at the Gahden the Lakahs fall tah the Celtics in 4 easy games!

…n' ehh… but yeah, yah know, so poohr fuckin' Frey, he gets knifed in the back by Goodell but then Mickey Ward winds up n' clocks Goodell right in the fuckin' face while at the same time Thor finally takes down the sehrpent but it sneezes a shit-ton'ah poison on him which ain't the same as bee'ah r'n so Thor can't handle it n' he fuckin' dies n' then Thor's kid the Green Mon-stah[128] comes back tah life n' it sprouts some legs n' stahts ram-

---

128 See page 30 of *Thor Begets the Green Monster* for more on Wally's unique and unusual parentage.

Vígríðr, more commonly known as Boston Common, is the plain at the center of the Hub of the Universe upon which the final world-shattering battle of Ragnarök will take place.

pagin' down Boylston Street like a crazy fuckin' wahr machine, squashin' evuhry evil fuckin' frost giant that crosses it's fuckin' path! But then the real crazy thing is that, while this is happenin', Odin gets eaten alive by the fuckin' wolf! I sweahr tah fuckin' God, that piece'ah-shit canine swallahs Odin whole like he's nothin' mohr 'en a soft fuckin' wad'ah peanut buttah ah somethin'. But then Teddy Williams[129] rises up from outtah the Pahk Street T-Station n' rips a homah straight through the wolf's

---

129 *The Prose Edda's Gylfaginning* and *The Poetic Edda's Völuspá* both attribute the slaughter of the wolf to Vidar rather than home-run slugger, Ted Williams. Vidar is Odin's son by the giantess, Grid, who in the Elder Eddas had assisted Thor by giving him special equipment when he was en route to visit the giant Geirrod, as described on page 100 in *Thor Wades through the Menstrual Fluid Fjord.*

fuckin' skull n' drops that bastahd like a non-rhotic R in an ovahdone sterotype…

… so then, uhhh, ok, so fuckin' Goodell—who truly, truly fuckin' hates himself—sets himself on fi'ah when he trips n' impales himself on his own fuckin' swohrd since no one likes him n' so now that whole fi'ah spreads like a fuckin' wild fi'ah 'cross the hub n' the entiyah univehrse buhrns tah a fuckin' crisp![130]

Yeah, yah know, since we've had such a drought this sum—Hhuhhh???

… n' so yeah, the entiyah fuckin' univehrse buhrns n' so ah'courhse all the Nova Scotians ahr all bawlin' their fuckin' eyes out 'cause there just went all their fuckin' Christmas trees n'—

YOU GOTTAH BE FUCKIN' KIDDIN' ME!!!!

Wha…..???

Uhhhggghhh……

THAT IS FUCKING BULLSHIT!!!!!!!!!

---

130 This fire is equivalent to the final cataclysmic supernova that ends all, or almost all life, in the ancient Norse known universe. The sudden re-ignition of an unknown and unnamed degenerate star by Goodell/Surt's sword causes a chain reaction of nuclear fusion and a subsequent gravitational collapse, ending all life known to inhabit the high-energy interstellar structure known as Yggdrasil with only very few exceptions. Yggdrasil itself is subjected to numerous fast-moving shock waves, that initiate a new phase of nucleosynthesis that makes the ancient wood of its intergalactic constituents groan and strain as it undergoes broad-range endothermic cosmic stress. Yggdrasil survives this cataclysmic event, albeit with a differentiated and new interstellar composition of chemical elements due to the supernova's cosmic ray spallation; its branches have shifted in the cosmic wind and it has radioactively grown a new, fourth asymptotic giant branch root. The fates of the long-duration gamma ray burst known as Níðhöggr the Dragon and the squirrel-like forbidden mechanism known as Ratatosk have not been specifically addressed by the primary sources, nor have they yet been adequately studied by scientists to comment on their fate at the time of this printing.

Jesus Christ…HOW THE FUCK?!?
Ugh…[131]

---

131 At this point in the recording, *The Impudent Edda* deteriorates
into a series of incoherent gurgles and expletives about the
goaltending of Tuuka Rask and the "douchebaggery" of the Saint
Louis Blues. As with many historical manuscripts, the incomplete-
ness leaves us only with the ability to speculate about the missing
material and we will never know exactly how the anonymous
scribe intended to formally end his Edda, but we can at least
attempt to fill the void with the knowledge that has been retained
in the Elder Eddas and thereby postulate a probable conclusion to
the events thus far described. Despite numerous deviations, omis-
sions, and new fabrications, *The Impudent Edda* has throughout
its course generally followed the same mythological story arc as
the Elder Eddas, so it remains likely that it would have continued
along this same trajectory, describing the same or similar events
and outcomes, though perhaps with some deviations.

The inferno started by Surt (or Goodell, in *The Impudent Edda*'s
version) rages throughout all the 9 Worlds, burning and killing
all. Or almost all. As the flames eventually subside, it comes to
be revealed that there are in fact a limited number of survivors.
Among these are Odin's sons Vidar and Vali and Thor's sons Modi
and Magni. Odin's previously dead sons, Brady/Balder and Hod
will survive and return from the depths of Hel where they sat out
the final battle between gods and monsters. Odin's brothers Vili
and Ve will also survive, as will Hoenir, who had been sent to live
among the Vanir as part of the two tribes of gods' truce agreement
in the early days following the war that was instigated when Odin
murdered a witch. Two humans who hid deep in the branches and
bark of Yggdrasil will also survive the universe cleansing-flames,
and they will repopulate the world. The sun will be reborn and the
world will grow good and green and new all over again. The fact
that the Elder Eddas contain a world-rebirth myth and that *The
Impudent Edda* does not can only lead one to contemplate that
present-day Boston sports fans are perhaps even more fatalistic
than the ancient Scandinavians had been.

Afterword

The recording of *The Impudent Edda* ends in a downward spiral of drunken stupor, characterized by increasingly frequent deviations from its description of Ragnarök that consistently involve the thrusting of hostile invectives upon the cohesive teamwork and frustratingly superior play of the 2019 Stanley Cup Finals Game 7 winners, the St. Louis Blues. After a final series of eloquently timed F-bombs, curses about the goaltending of Tuuka Rask in the final minutes of the game, and expressions of general disgust and a desire to go home, the unknown orator then asks the name of his equally unknown drinking partner, whom he has presumably never before met (and who may very well have been an unwilling recipient of the archaic knowledge revealed), and then the recording abruptly ends, the electronic device having reached the full extent of its available hard-disc space. We can only speculate as to how the electronic device containing this invaluable trove of Norse lore ended up in the dark corner of a dank alleyway that appears to only ever be frequented by late-night inebriated patrons of local neighborhood drinking establishments when in desperate need of relieving their full and aching bladders.

In the course of its telling, *The Impudent Edda* corroborates many details found in the Elder Eddas, and provides many new and heretofore unknown details that have expanded our knowledge of ancient Norse mythological beliefs. Stories such as those about Thor's fathering of the Green Monster or Odin's passing out shit-faced on the steps of the Boston Public Library have granted us new insight into the world that the Norse gods inhabited. They have also increased our understanding of the sorts of behavioral characteristics and interactions with which the gods engaged one another. Generally, these new revelations remain consistent with and support the characteristics of the gods that have been propagated by the Elder Eddas for centuries.

While *The Impudent Edda* has generally strengthened our knowledge concerning many ancient stories of the Norse gods and contributed a few new ones, it has also completely neglected some of the most prominent stories described in the earlier sources. *The Impudent Edda* offers no new knowledge, for example, about the story of Thor's journey to Giant Land in which he attempts to display feats of strength and drinking prowess but is instead made to look like a fool, or about his battle with the evil giant, Hrungnir, in which he emerges the obvious victor but with a piece of a whetstone lodged eternally in his head forever after, or about Loki's "flyting," in which Loki hurls insults at each and every one of the gods and goddesses after the death of Brady/Balder and immediately prior to his subsequent capture and torture. This myth, contained within the *Lokasenna* in *The Poetic Edda*, plays a particularly pivotal role in advancing its narrative towards Ragnarök, but goes essentially unobserved in both *The Prose Edda* and *The Impudent Edda*.

None of which is entirely surprising, since by nature, mythology has always been ever-evolving and never 100% consistent. We have long thought Norse mythology to be stuck in a state of stasis ever since the conversion of the northlands to Christianity in the medieval period, but now we have reason and sufficient literary evidence to believe that this may never have actually been the case. The stories of the dread god, Odin, his boisterous son, Thor, and all the others have lived on, not only in the most popular forms of pop culture (albeit with varying degrees of substance and genuineness) such as those evidenced by the comics/films of Marvel Comics or the novels of Neil Gaiman, but also in terms of the actual religious beliefs that adhere to and further shape the lives and behaviors of the gods.

With the rise of contemporary Ásatrú and its increasing acceptance by larger swaths of society, we may again, perhaps even someday soon, greet another revolutionary breakthrough in our collective knowledge of Norse mythology. But until the next great discovery is made, let us rest with some degree of contentment with the new, invaluable knowledge that *The Impudent Edda* has bestowed upon us.

"The society of Boston was and is quite uncivilized, but refined beyond the point of civilization."

—T.S. Eliot

Index

mid-menstruation, sits on a levitating chair in Geirrod's goat shed: 101; squishes Gjalp and Greip to death, slays Geirrod with a hot ember: 102; drives his goats to the Green Line parking lot: 103; rides the Green Line downtown with Loki, visits the New England Aquarium with Loki: 104; flips out at T Station: 105; gets really excited to throw shit at Brady: 107; drives to Nashua to purchase hard liquor: 110; kicks a dwarf into a fire: 114; gets impatient with Loki's swimming: 122; dives into river rapids head-first, has whetsone lodged in his skull, catches Loki in fish-form by the tail: 123; drinks two kegs of stout, goes binge-drinking in downtown Boston: 124; passes out drunk on the streets of Boston: 127; wakes up hung-over: 129; wants a breakfast sandwich, breaks into Dunkin' Donuts, cries himself to sleep: 130; eats frozen hash browns: 137; kills Jörmundgandr, killed by Jörmundgandr: 137

Thrym, giant with Thor's hammer visited by Loki as a falcon, demands to marry Freyja: 69; impressed by Thor's unlady-like appetite, almost kisses Thor: 71; killed by Thor: 72

Thrymheim, freezing Quebec-like home of Skadi hated by Njord: 67

Transmogrifier, god particle altering device, used by Loki to shape-shift into falcon form: 62; used by Fafnir to shape-shift into dragon form: 82; Frigg's stolen by Loki: 97

Tyr, one-handed war god, cruises the backwoods with Fenrir in the front passenger seat: 53; puts his hand in Fenrir's mouth: 57; suggests visiting his father Hymir: 85; steals Hymir's beer cauldron with Thor: 90

Vali, son of Loki, brother of Nari/Narfi, turned into a wolf and mauls Nari/Narfi: 125

Vali, son of Odin, survives Ragnarök: 131

Valhalla, Odin's glorious hall of the slain: 135

Vanaheim, where the sex gods live: 14; looks like Berlin in 1945: 17

Vanir, the sex gods: 14; attack Asgard in retaliation for Odin's witch murder: 17

Ve, brother of Odin who helps murder Ymir: 6; survives Ragnarök: 140

Vidar, son of Odin and Grid, kills Fenrir: 138; survives Ragnarök: 140

Image Credits

PAGE 23
Kam (enkelkam, a3) av ben/horn
SHM Object Identification #269167
Photo by Christer Åhlin, 2011
Historiska Museet Stockholm
Reprinted in accordance with CC BY 2.5 SE
https://historiska.se/upptack-historien/object/269167-kam-enkelkam-a3-av-ben-horn/

PAGE 26
Sövestad-runesten (Krageholm)
Photo by Erik Moltke, 1939
Nationalmuseet Danmark
Reprinted in accordance with CC BY SA 2.0
https://samlinger.natmus.dk/DMR/asset/5752

PAGE 29
Agassiz Road Duck House
Photo by Rowdy Geirsson, 2019

PAGE 30
Lansdowne Street
Photo by Rowdy Geirsson, 2019

PAGE 36
Leonard P. Zakim Bunker Hill Memorial Bridge
Photo by Rowdy Geirsson, 2019

PAGE 41
Det længste guldhorn fra Gallehus (kopi)
Object Identification #18964
Photo by Roberto Fortuna and Kira Ursem, 2007
Nationalmuseet Danmark
Reprinted in accordance with CC BY SA 2.0
https://samlinger.natmus.dk/DO/asset/2869

PAGE 45
Hänge (freja) av silver
SHM Object Identification #107873
Photo by Gabriel Hildebrand, 2011
Historiska Museet Stockholm
Reprinted in accordance with CC BY 2.5 SE
https://historiska.se/upptack-historien/object/107873-hange-freja-av-silver/

PAGE 53
White Mountain National Forest
Photo by Rowdy Geirsson, 2019

PAGE 56
Islands of Casco Bay
Photo by Rowdy Geirsson, 2019

PAGE 61
New England Camp Ground
Photo by Rowdy Geirsson, 2019

PAGE 72
Hänge (torshammare) av silver
SHM Object Identification #106659
Photo by Gabriel Hildebrand, 2011
Historiska Museet Stockholm
Reprinted in accordance with CC BY 2.5 SE
https://historiska.se/upptack-historien/
object/106659-hange-torshammare-av-silver/

PAGE 74
Park Bench in Boston Common
Photo by Rowdy Geirsson, 2019

PAGE 76
McGreevey's
Photo by Rowdy Geirsson, 2019

PAGE 79
Statyett (statyett av frö) av brons
SHM Object Identification #109037
Photo by Gabriel Hildebrand, 2011
Historiska Museet Stockholm
Reprinted in accordance with CC BY 2.5 SE
https://historiska.se/upptack-historien/object/109037-
statyett-statyett-av-fro-av-brons/

PAGE 83
Parking Garage in Boston
Photo by Rowdy Geirsson, 2019

PAGE 91
Dyrehoved, ukendt findested
Object Identification #C31157
Photo by John Lee, 2005
Nationalmuseet Danmark
Reprinted in accordance with CC BY SA 2.0
https://samlinger.natmus.dk/DO/asset/1606

PAGE 94
Bobby Orr Statue
Photo by Rowdy Geirsson, 2019

PAGE 98
Original Filene's and Filene's Basement Location
Photo by Rowdy Geirsson, 2019

PAGE 104
New England Aquarium
Photo by Rowdy Geirsson, 2019

PAGE 110
Carving, Oosik
Object Identification #UAM:EH:UA99-018-0115
Courtesty of University of Alaska Museum of the North
Photo by Mahriena Ellanna
http://arctos.database.museum/guid/UAM:EH:UA99-018-0115

PAGE 116
Tjängvidestenen
SHM Object Identification #108203
Photo by Ola Myrin, 2017
Historiska Museet Stockholm
Reprinted in accordance with CC BY 2.5 SE
http://mis.historiska.se/mis/sok/bild.asp?uid=446023

PAGE 121
New England River Rapids
Photo by Rowdy Geirsson, 2019

PAGE 126
New England Holocaust Memorial
Photo by Rowdy Geirsson, 2019

PAGE 131
Dunkin' Donuts in Downtown Boston
Photo by Rowdy Geirsson, 2019

PAGE 134
Charles Street Manholes
Photo by Rowdy Geirsson, 2019

PAGE 136
Longfellow Bridge
Photo by Rowdy Geirsson, 2019

PAGE 138
Boston Common
Photo by Rowdy Geirsson, 2019

Additional Resources

The following list provides additional references for further study for anyone wishing to delve deeper into the world of the Vikings and the Norse gods to whom they adhered. In addition to primary written sources and historical studies, a handful of important cultural auditory contributions have been included as well. Many of these auditory resources are simply a single archetypal example by a given artist who has actually produced multiple, analytical works of relevance.

Overall, this directory is not meant to be comprehensive, but rather an informative starting point for anyone who may have acquired a new interest in a very old subject matter.

Amon Amarth. 2002. *Versus the World*. Metal Blade Records.

Anderson, Poul. 1997. *War of the Gods*. Tor Fantasy.

Anonymous. 1977. *Beowulf*. Translated by Howell D. Chickering. Anchor Books.

Anonymous. 2011. *The Elder Edda*. Translated by Andy Orchard. Penguin Classics.

Anonymous. 1962. *The Poetic Edda*. Translated by Lee M. Hollander. University of Texas Press.

Anonymous. 2005. *The Saga of Grettir the Strong*. Translated by Bernard Scudder. Penguin Books.

Anonymous. 1998. *The Saga of King Hrolf Kraki*. Translated by Jesse L. Byock. Penguin.

Anonymous. 1990. *Saga of the Volsungs: The Norse Epic of Sigurd the Dragon Slayer*. Translated by Jesse L. Byock. University of California Press.

Bathory. 1990. *Hammerheart*. Noise Records.

Brown, Nancy Marie. 2012. *Song of the Vikings: Snorri and the Making of Norse Myths*. Palgrave Macmillan

Crossley-Holland, Kevin. 1981. *The Norse Myths*. Pantheon Books.

Davidson, H. R. Ellis. 1964. *Gods and Myths of Northern Europe*. Penguin.

Fejd. 2013. *Nagelfar*. Napalm Records.

Fitzhugh, William W., and Elisabeth I. Ward, eds. 2000. *Vikings: The North Atlantic Saga*. Smithsonian Institution Press.

Haywood, John. 1995. *The Penguin Historical Atlas of the Vikings*. Penguin.

Kershaw, Nora. 1921. "The Tháttr of Sörli" in *Stories and Ballads of the Far Past*, Translated from the Norse (Icelandic and Faroese) with Introductions and Notes. University of Cambridge Press.

Månegarm. 2015. *Månegarm*. Napalm Records.

Näsström, Britt-Marie. 1996. "Freyja and Frigg—Two Aspects of the Great Goddess" in *Pentikäinen*, Juha (ed.), Shamanism and Northern Ecology. De Gruyter.

O'Donoghue, Heather. 2007. *From Asgard to Valhalla: The Remarkable History of the Norse Myths*. I.B. Tauris & Co.

Skálmöld. 2010. *Baldur*. Napalm Records.

Smiley, Jane et al. 2000. *The Sagas of Icelanders*. Penguin.

Sturluson, Snorri. 2005. *The Prose Edda*. Translated by Jesse Byock. Penguin Classics.

Sturluson, Snorri. 1990. *Heimskringla*. Edited and translated by Erling Monsen and A.H. Smith. Dover Publications.

Therion. 2001. *Secret of the Runes*. Nuclear Blast.

Týr. 2006. *Ragnarok*. Napalm Records.

Unleashed. 1993. *Across the Open Sea*. Century Media Records.

Wardruna. 2009. *Runaljod - Gap Var Ginnunga*. Indie Recordings/ Fimbulljóð Productions.

NORSE MYTHOLOGY FOR BOSTONIANS

McSweeney's Internet Tendency
NORSE MYTHOLOGY FOR BOSTONIANS
ROWDY GEIRSSON

In 2019, abandoned smartphone was found partially buried beneath layers of sediment and urine in a South Boston alleyway. This forgotten relic was soon revealed to contain a remarkable audio-text describing in great detail the religious beliefs of ancient Scandinavia. Dubbed *The Impudent Edda*, this oral manuscript was transcribed and released to the general public as *Norse Mythology for Bostonians* in early 2020—the very book that you now hold in your hands, dear reader.

During the global lockdown that followed the book's release, archaeologists, historians, and philologists continued to study the audio text as well as the device itself, now known simply as the *Codex Bostonia*. These researchers eventually uncovered an additional stash of hidden audio files stored in a previously secret location on the phone's memory card. Beginning in the fall of 2022, these recently recovered myths are being made available to the public at McSweeney's on a rolling basis as they are uncovered.

The breadth of these lost myths' arcane lore, the depth of their spiritual insights, and the poignancy of their poetic revelations confirm that the collective audio texts of the *Codex Bostonia* remain the single most important contribution to our knowledge of pre-Christian Scandinavian religious beliefs to have emerged in a millennium.

NORSE MYTHOLOGY FOR BOSTONIANS

Illustration from the uncovered lost myth, *Odin Sends Freyja a Dick Pic* (first released to the public in August of 2022), by Matt Smith

BEAVIS & BUTT-HEAD STARRING ODIN & THOR

Metal Sucks

BEAVIS AND BUTT-HEAD STARRING ODIN AND THOR
ROWDY GEIRSSON

AN EXCERPT FROM PART 3: FREYJA IS HOT BUT FIRE IS COOL

[ODIN and FREYJA presently stand fixed in place in the middle of the austere and overly-spacious, mostly empty room and watch as THOR, having transformed into THOR-NHOLIO after impulsively consuming FREYJA's divine birth control pills, mindlessly wanders around with his cape pulled backwards up over his head.

Frustrated by having been duped by ODIN into visiting Asgard to retrieve a necklace that he doesn't even possess, FREYJA clenches her jaw and bears an expression of total disgust upon her face. FREYJA's assorted rings, necklaces, bracelets, and other items of jewelry sway slightly with the fall and rise of each of her angry breaths. Oblivious to FREYJA's foul mood, THOR-NHOLIO continues to recklessly brandish his mighty hammer, Mjölnir, like a madman and mutters maniacally as he roams the room.]

THOR-NHOLIO: Heh heh hmm. I am Thor-nholio! Heh hmmm hmmmm. Hammer. Heh heh heh. Hammer. Hammer. Hmmmmmmmm heh heh heh hammer hmm.

ODIN: Huh huh huh.

THOR-NHOLIO: Heh heh. Hammer. Heh heh hmmm. Do you have goat-mead for my lung-hole? Heh heh. Hammer! Heh heh heh hmmmm hammer hammer hammer hammer!

FREYJA [to ODIN]: What the fuck is wrong with the two of you?

ODIN: Uhhh… we're cool. Huh huh.

THOR-NHOLIO [turning and walking back towards ODIN and FREYJA, still wildly flailing Mjölnir around]: Hammer! Heh heh hmmmmmmm hmm hammer! Hammer! Hmmmm.

FREYJA: Okay, that's it. I'm leaving.

read more

BEAVIS & BUTT-HEAD STARRING ODIN & THOR

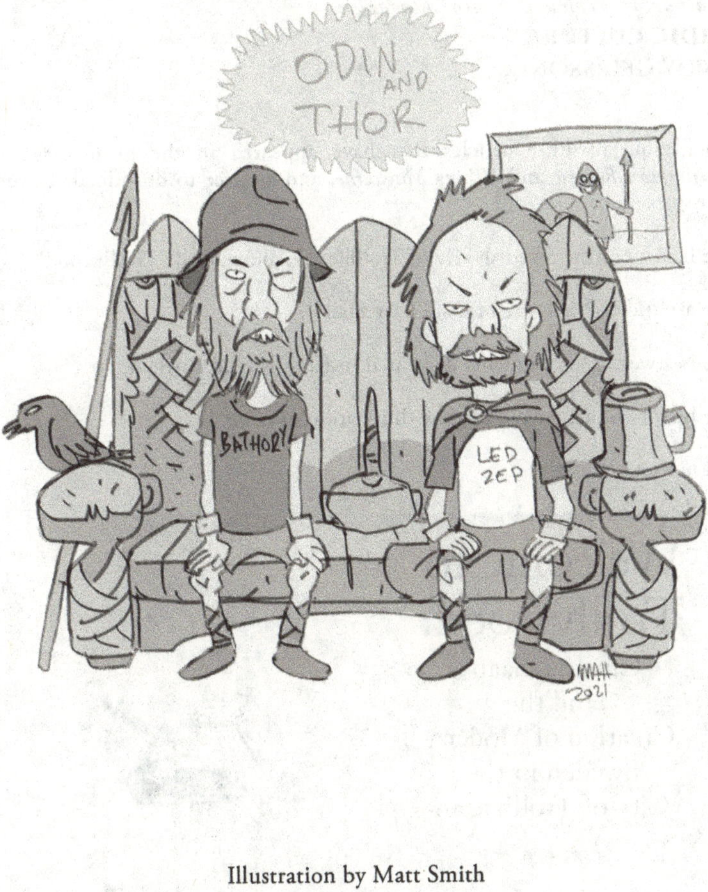

Illustration by Matt Smith

www.metalsucks.net/category/misadventures-in-heavy-metalling/

NORDIC CULTURE

Sign of metro
station in Oslo

Taking the T

What do the underground transit systems of Boston, Stockholm and Oslo all have in common? They have a nearly identical visual identity, the T-shaped symbol, that helps riders navigate the cities with ease.

BY ROWDY GEIRSSON

www.scandinavianaggression.com/magazine-articles

BARBARIAN LORD

Graphic Novel and Stand-Alone Issues
BARBARIAN LORD
MATT SMITH

"He is hard to get along with."

Equal parts Egil Skallagrimsson and Thundarr the Barbarian, Barbarian Lord is a character borne of the unvarnished tone of the medieval Icelandic Sagas with a heavy infusion of 1980's barbarian cartoons. 176 pages of grim determination may be enjoyed with the noble brute via the Barbarian Lord graphic novel, released by Clarion Books, and shorter, but equally grim stand-alone issues are available from the artist directly.

http://matt-illustration.squarespace.com/barbarian-lord-1

METAL QUEST

Wicked Heavy Graphic Novel
METAL QUEST
TOM PAPPALARDO & MATT SMITH

"-33 1/3: The RPM of the Beast"

Two headbangers are transported to a strange world of demons, trapped souls, and the mysterious heavy metal band Infinitaur. Will the Ghods rise from their slumber? Can Tracy and Rhawn work together to summon their Inner Rock? A work-in-progress comic/graphic novel by Tom Pappalardo and Matt Smith.

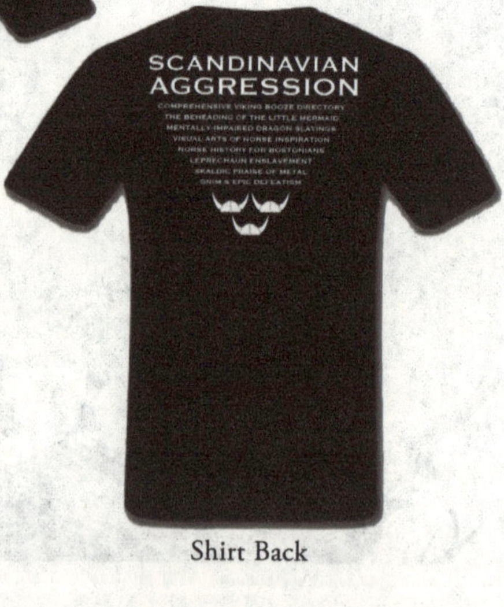

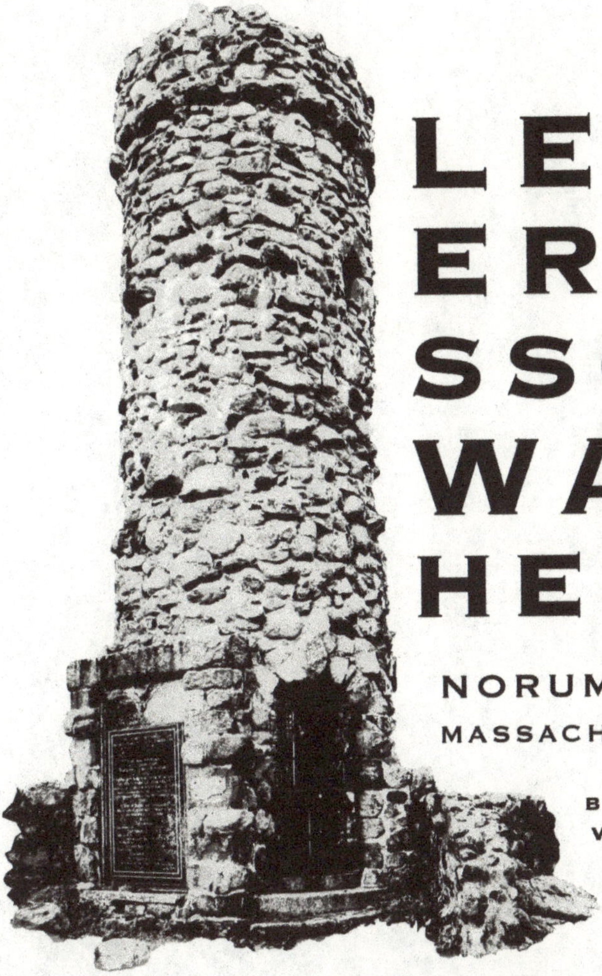

LEIF ERIKSSON WAS HERE

NORUMBEGA
MASSACHUSETTS

BOSTON'S VINLAND SINCE 1889

SCANDINAVIAN AGGRESSION

COMPREHENSIVE VIKING BOOZE DIRECTORY
THE BEHEADING OF THE LITTLE MERMAID
MENTALLY-IMPAIRED DRAGON SLAYINGS
VISUAL ARTS OF NORSE INSPIRATION
NORSE HISTORY FOR BOSTONIANS
LEPRECHAUN ENSLAVEMENT
SKALDIC PRAISE OF METAL
GRIM & EPIC DEFEATISM

Front and Back Design Enlargements

47900CB00011B/2862